RETURN to ROAR

JENNY MCLACHLAN

EGMONT

EGMONT

We bring stories to life

First published in Great Britain in 2020 by Egmont Books

An imprint of HarperCollins*Publishers*
1 London Bridge Street
London SE1 9GF

egmontbooks.co.uk

ISBN 978 1 4052 9502 4

A CIP catalogue record for this title is available from the British Library

70069/004

Printed and bound in Great Britain by CPI Group

Typeset by Avon DataSet Ltd, Alcester, Warwickshire

MIX
Paper from
responsible sources
FSC™ C007454

For wild and wonderful Mara

MITCH

ARchie PLAYGO

TANGLED

ROAR

the END →

the CROW's Nest

the BAD SIDE

DUNGUN

est

by ROSE
and ARTHUR

CHAPTER 1

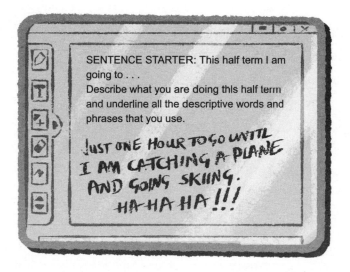

SENTENCE STARTER: This half term I am
going to . . .
Describe what you are doing this half term
and underline all the descriptive words and
phrases that you use.

JUST ONE HOUR TO GO UNTIL
I AM CATCHING A PLANE
AND GOING SKIING.
HA-HA HA !!!

The work on the interactive whiteboard suggests Miss
Kimble isn't taking this lesson very seriously. Who
can blame her? We're about to break up for half-term and
there's a very relaxed atmosphere in the room.

Music is playing, pens and rubbers are flying around,
and everyone is chatting. Miss Kimble is frantically tidying
her desk because – as she keeps telling us – she has a plane

to catch, and my sister is plaiting Harriet Scott's hair. No one is doing any work.

Except me.

I pick up my pen and start to write. Miss Kimble isn't the only one going somewhere exciting this holiday.

This half-term I am going to visit the Land of Roar with my twin sister, Rose. We're not sure exactly where Roar is, but to get there we have to crawl through <u>an ancient, rusty, folding camp bed</u> in our grandad's attic. The camp bed isn't a <u>glamorous</u> portal to a fantasy world, but it works and that's what matters.

Once we've arrived in Roar we'll hang out with my best friend: Wininja. <u>Win is as stealthy as a fox, as flexible as a rubber band and as magical as a wand</u> because he is half ninja and half wizard.

After we've explored Roar we will fly a dragon. Flying a dragon <u>is cooler than a slushy</u> although <u>their bodies feel as hot as an oven.</u> At some point we will visit the Crow's Nest which is this <u>terrifying</u> castle in the middle of the sea. A gang of wild girls live there, but it used to belong to our nemesis, Crowky.

Crowky is a <u>total villain</u>. <u>He is also as clever as a crow and as creepy as a scarecrow.</u> This is because he's a scarecrow with crow wings (although his wings might not be working right now because last time we were in Roar a dragon set fire to them – long story).

I'm also looking forward to swimming with some <u>heavily-tattooed merfolk</u>. The only reason I'm doing this work is to distract me because I'm DESPERATE for the bell to ring. When it does I'm going to _zoom_ round to Grandad's (_as fast as a cheetah_) and then the adventure will begin!

'Arthur, what _are_ you doing?' I look up to see my sister standing over to me.

'What?' I say, covering my work. 'Miss Kimble's never going to mark it, is she? She's going skiing.'

Rose slips into the seat next to me and puts a cake tin on the desk. 'Yes, but what if someone else reads it? They'll think you're crazy!'

I grin. 'But I'm not, am I, Rose? We're actually going back to Roar. Today!'

'_Shhh!_' She looks around, to make sure no one's listening.

My sister hates talking about Roar at school, but right now I'm too excited to follow her rules. 'Rose, this evening we could be flying a dragon!'

She can't help herself. She has to smile. 'I know. I just wish we could be there right now!'

She says these words with such passion that I'm surprised. Like me Rose loves Roar, but she also loves it here at Langton Academy. We've only just started, but she's already got this massive gang of friends who she hangs out with all day, and then all night via her phone. By contrast, I've made one friend, Adam Zeng. He's great, but right now he's having his tonsils out, which is why I'm sitting on my own.

'When we get to Roar what do you want to do first?' I say.

3

Rose looks at me like I'm stupid. 'Go and see Mitch of course.'

If Win is my best friend in Roar, then Mitch is Rose's. She's a merwitch who lives on her very own island, but the last time we were there we discovered she'd gone missing. Just before we left we saw something swimming in the sea and Rose was convinced it was Mitch, but really it could have been anything. So I say, 'Rose, you know Mitch might not be back yet?'

She hugs the cake tin to her. 'She has to be! Mitch disappeared because I forgot about her, but I can remember her so clearly now: her webbed fingers, her tattoos, her hair. It was bright blue.'

'The colour of bubble-gum ice cream,' I say.

She smiles. 'Exactly!'

'But, Rose, if Mitch isn't back, there are loads of other amazing things we can do.'

She shakes her head stubbornly. 'No. I only want to see Mitch. I've got so much to tell her.' Then she glances across the room at her new friends. They're gathered round Harriet Scott – the loudest of the group – who is saying something so shocking the other girls' mouths are hanging open.

Rose's gang look identical, and not just because of their gaping mouths. They're all wearing their ties short and chubby and their socks pulled up high, and every one of them, including Rose, has their hair in one long plait.

Rose says they do all this matching stuff to show what good friends they are. Rose's fingers drum on the cake tin. That's another way they show what good friends they are: by baking.

'Can I have a cake?' I say.

Rose opens the tin, revealing rows of perfect cupcakes. Each one has a different emoji face iced on it. 'Sorry, I've not got enough.'

Suddenly Harriet's voice rings out across the classroom. 'Rose, come here! We want to show you something!'

Rose hesitates. I guess she doesn't want to leave me on my own. 'I'm fine,' I say, and she gives me a grateful smile before shooting off.

I look at my watch. Just six minutes to go. My heart squeezes with excitement. I'm not sure how much more of this I can take. In front of me, Tariq bends over his bag and shoves half an egg sandwich in his mouth. We're breaking up at lunchtime, but obviously he can't wait.

The eggy smell drifts over me, and I shut my eyes and breathe it in. *Dragons*, I think, and in a flash I'm back in Roar, flying high over the Bottomless Ocean on Vlad. Waves crash below us and Vlad sends a jet of fire rolling towards me along with the smell of sulphur.

Something hits my head and I open my eyes to see a rubber sitting on the desk. From across the room Harriet calls out, 'Sorry, Arthur. I was aiming for Tariq!'

Miss Kimble looks up and realises that her classroom has

descended into chaos. 'Right,' she says, clapping her hands. 'Who'd like to share one of their descriptive sentences with the class?' Everyone falls quiet, even Harriet. Then, like a dragon sighting its prey, Miss Kimble's eyes lock on to me. 'Arthur Trout, let's hear one of yours.'

'Umm . . .' I swallow and desperately try to find a sentence that doesn't involve anything magical. '*I'm also looking forward to swimming,*' I read, skipping the bit about heavily-tattooed merfolk.

Miss Kimble frowns. 'Well it's a sentence, but I wouldn't exactly call it *descriptive*. Let's have another one.'

Rose turns and shoots massive evils in my direction. I'm seconds away from the end of term and I'm about to get into trouble. 'Ahh . . .' I say.

And then, quite literally, I'm saved by the bell.

The classroom erupts with noise as chairs are scraped back, books are stuffed into bags and coats are pulled on. 'Take your work home with you!' shouts Miss Kimble, as she rushes towards the door. 'You can finish it during half-term WHILE I'M SKIING!'

I crumple up my piece of paper and stuff it in my pocket. I don't need to write about Roar, because finally, after weeks of planning and waiting and dreaming, I'm going back.

CHAPTER 2

While Rose gives out her cakes, I join the crush of students heading out of school.

Mum's parked exactly where she said she'd be and seeing as Rose isn't here I take the front seat.

'Hey, Arthur!' Mum says, giving my hair a vigorous ruffle. 'Looking forward to staying with your grandad?'

'Yeah,' I say, fighting back the enormous grin that's threatening to burst across my face. Mum and Dad are pretty cool, but there's no way they would agree to me and Rose having a mini-break in a fantasy world. They think that while they're walking in Scotland, Rose and I will be having a relaxing week at Grandad's. To keep Mum believing this I start telling her all the things we're planning to do. 'Grandad's promised to take us fishing,' I say, 'and out on our bikes, oh, and he's finished the den in the attic so Rose and I don't have to share a room any more.'

'Speaking of Rose, where is she?' Mum rubs a circle

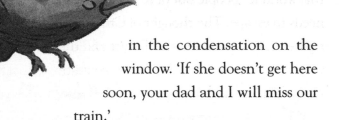

in the condensation on the window. 'If she doesn't get here soon, your dad and I will miss our train.'

'I'll go and find her,' I say, unclipping my seatbelt and jumping out of the car. I can't believe Rose would rather give out cakes than get to Roar!

I'm running across the playground, when a dark shape flies past my face. I gasp and hold my breath until I realise that the shape is just a crow swooping down on a half-eaten panini. My heart continues to thud as I walk into school. I have a lot of moments like this: I catch sight of someone wearing a black coat or I hear the flutter of wings, and a flash of fear rushes through me. A few days ago I actually yelled in history when a seagull tapped on the window.

There's a good reason why I'm so jumpy.

The last time I saw Crowky – burnt and broken on the deck of the *Raven* – he was wearing my grandad's 'NO PROB-LLAMA!' T-shirt. Although Crowky doesn't know it, objects from this world let people out of Roar, and that T-shirt is all he needs to escape. The thought of Crowky crawling into the tunnel in Roar wearing the T-shirt and then appearing in Grandad's attic is horrible. What would he do first? Stuff Grandad or come looking for me and Rose?

At first I didn't mention the T-shirt to Rose and Grandad. To be honest, I wanted to forget all about it, but then one Saturday a rook landed on Grandad's bird table and I was so freaked out I dropped my hot chocolate. Rose asked what was wrong, and I blurted out that Crowky still had Grandad's T-shirt. Unlike me, they weren't bothered about it. Rose said it was falling apart when we last saw Crowky, and that it would be at the bottom of the Bottomless Ocean by now, and Grandad agreed with her. But I'm not so sure . . .

I turn a corner and almost run into Harriet and the rest of Rose's friends. Their arms are linked and Harriet's laughing. 'Where's Rose?' I say.

Harriet's smile disappears. 'Arthur, it's terrible. She's dropped her cakes!'

'I still think we should help tidy up,' says Nisha. I've known Nisha since primary school, and right now I can tell she's worried.

Harriet glances at her phone. 'We haven't got time. If we miss the bus, we miss the film. Fish understands.' Then she walks past me and one by one the others follow. 'Bye, Arthur,' she calls over her shoulder. 'Have a good half-term!'

I find Rose on her hands and knees in the Geography corridor. Her cupcakes are everywhere: mashed into the floor, squished into lockers, and even smeared across a noticeboard.

'What happened?' I say. 'It looks like they exploded!'

Rose shakes her head. She looks totally miserable. 'Some Year Elevens went past and the tin got knocked out of my hands. Then the cakes got chucked around.'

I start to scoop up broken bits of cake, dropping them in the bin. 'The others should have helped you pick them up,' I say.

Rose shrugs. 'They didn't have time. They've got a bus to catch.'

Still, I think, *they should have helped*, but I don't say this out loud because Rose looks like she's about to cry, and if there's one thing Rose hates doing it's crying. So instead I grab more handfuls of cake, trying to get the job done as quickly as possible.

Soon we're walking out of school and I'm eating an almost complete cupcake that I found resting on a radiator. 'This one tastes great, Rose.'

She gives me a quick smile. 'Thanks, Arthur.'

I crunch down on one of the silver balls. 'How come Harriet calls you Fish?'

She rolls her eyes. 'Because our surname's Trout, you idiot.'

'Oh yeah! So can I call you Fish?'

'No,' she says, giving me a shove.

When we bundle into Mum's car we're out of breath and laughing. We raced for the front seat and Rose won, of course. 'About time,' says Mum. 'Did your friends like their cakes, Rose?'

There's this moment of silence where I know Rose doesn't want to go into the whole cake-dropping business, so I say, 'I had one. It tasted amazing.'

Then Adele comes on the radio, distracting Mum.

As we drive out of town towards the coast, Mum sings along to the radio and Rose rests her head on the window. I lick icing off my fingers, and I try to ignore the scarecrow I've just spotted standing all alone in the middle of a field.

CHAPTER 3

'Right, lecture time,' says Mum as we turn into Grandad's driveway. 'Do your teeth at least once a day, eat fruit or vegetables twice a day and, Rose, don't live on your phone.'

Overgrown bushes and trees scrape the sides of the car. As usual, Rose's phone is in her hand. 'Actually, Mum,' she says, 'I'm going to turn it off for the holiday and have a complete digital detox.'

'*What?*' Mum's so shocked she almost drives into Grandad's birdbath. Rose loves her phone. She can get through a whole day without looking at me, but she looks at her phone about a thousand times.

Rose shrugs like it's no big deal. 'I watched this thing on YouTube about how bad phones are for your happiness so I thought I'd have a break.'

Mum stops the car and throws her arms round Rose. 'I am *so* proud of you!'

Over Mum's shoulder Rose catches my eye and grins.

Then she says, 'Maybe you should do the same, Mum. You and Dad are going to Scotland to get away from it all, so why not turn your phones off too? If there's a problem Grandad can ring your hotel.'

'If you can do it, then so can we,' says Mum, squeezing Rose even tighter. 'My little girl is so wise!'

Cunning more like, but I have to admire Rose's quick thinking. We want to stay in Roar for the whole of half-term and now we don't need to worry about Mum or Dad wanting to speak to us.

A bang makes me jump. Grandad's sneaked out of his house and is now squishing his face against my window.

Mum is horrified. 'Is he actually *licking* the glass?'

He is, and it's hilarious. Rose and I jump out of the car and are immediately pulled into one of Grandad's prickly hugs. Grandad's not a big fan of shaving. Or trousers. Just like every other day of the year, he's wearing shorts and sandals that show off his large gnarly toenails.

'Not long now,' he says, and for a moment the three of us are lost in the excitement of our shared secret.

Mum beeps the car horn. 'Grab your bags, twins!'

We pull them out of the boot. They're full of clothes we won't wear and books we won't read, but we had to pack them so Mum and Dad didn't get suspicious.

After Mum's done an awkward six-point turn, she leans out of the window and fixes us with a stern look. 'Make sure you don't spend the week lounging around.'

I shake my head. 'We're not going to do any lounging, are we Rose?'

'No way. We're going to go swimming –'

'And cycling and . . . jogging!' I say.

For a moment Mum narrows her eyes suspiciously, then she says, 'Fine, just don't watch too much TV.'

Then, with a beep and a final wave, she drives away.

We all let out a sigh of relief.

'Well, she didn't say anything about *not* riding dragons,' says Grandad.

'Or hanging out with ninja wizards,' I say.

'Or jumping off waterfalls,' Rose adds.

Grandad throws his hands up in the air and does a big belly laugh. 'Looks like you're good to go then!'

CHAPTER 4

'Ta-da!' Grandad throws open the door to the attic. It's incredible. He's transformed the dusty room into the den he promised us. There's a squishy sofa, beanbags, books and games; there's even a popcorn machine. Grandad's put framed photos on the wall of him and Nani in Mauritius, and I spot two china dodos that belonged to Nani. The whole room looks cosy and cool, and a massive improvement on the junk-stuffed attic.

Rose and I run around, bouncing on the sofa and looking in drawers. Rose's old rocking horse, Prosecco, is sitting in front of the window giving me evils. No change there then. The Prosecco in Roar hates me too, only he's more of a threat because he's an actual stallion with large teeth and a boy-stinging tail.

'Arthur, come and look at this,' says Rose. She's found a trunk and it's full of our old toys. I pull out a ninja costume that looks just like the robes Win wears, a bag of pirate Lego and then a red plastic dragon.

'I thought you'd taken all this to the charity shop,' I say to Grandad.

He shrugs. 'It seemed a shame to throw it out.'

I know what he means. It was playing with these toys that led to Roar appearing inside the camp bed. We don't know how it happened, or why some games came to life in Roar while others stayed firmly in the real world, but these toys are where it all began.

Rose carefully folds a mermaid's tail and puts it back in the trunk. She looks round the attic. 'I love it all, Grandad!'

'You've not seen the best bit yet,' he says, then he bends down and flicks a switch. A string of fairy lights starts to flash over one of the eaves, and I see that tucked inside, covered in Nani's silky sari, is the folding camp bed. Its boxy shape makes a shiver run through me.

Grandad smiles proudly. 'I thought a magical portal deserved a special place to live,' he says, and then, like a magician, he whips off the sari.

I stare at the camp bed's familiar flowery mattress and rusty springs. The plastic headboard reflects the twinkling fairy lights. I run my hands over the words I scratched into the headboard years ago –

ENTUR HEER FOR THE LANED OF ROAR!!!

– and my stomach knots with excitement. Soon we'll be crawling into the mattress. Soon we'll be in Roar!

'I polished the headboard and oiled the wheels,' says

16

Grandad, pulling the bed into the middle of the room.

'But you haven't opened it, have you?' asks Rose. She's always believed that opening the bed will make everything inside disappear. We don't know if this is true, but it's not something we ever want to test out.

'I've not opened it, or even put my head in there,' he says. 'I'm only crawling into that camp bed if you two don't come back next Sunday.'

I don't blame Grandad for not wanting to go inside the bed. It was only a few months ago that Crowky dragged him out of my hands, through the bed and into Roar. Crowky took Grandad to the Crow's Nest where he stuffed him by pressing his twiggy fingers down on his body and squeezing the life out of him. Grandad would have stayed like that forever – a lifeless scarecrow – if Rose and I hadn't got to him in time.

Just thinking about Crowky makes the excited tingle in my stomach turn into a knot of worry. I take a step back from the bed as if I'm expecting Crowky's hand to appear and grab hold of me, or worse, grab hold of Grandad.

'You all right, Arthur?' says Grandad.

I force myself to smile. 'Yeah . . . just excited.'

'No he's not,' says Rose. 'He's worried about the T-shirt.' My sister can read my mind. It's a twin thing. She knows when I'm happy, sad, worried or lying. It's really annoying.

Grandad pats my shoulder. 'You don't need to worry about that old thing, Arthur. It was falling to bits before

17

Crowky got his hands on it. It was my painting T-shirt, remember?'

'Plus Crowky hasn't got a clue what it can do,' adds Rose. 'As far as he's concerned it's just an old T-shirt, not some key that will magically let him out of Roar and into this world!'

Her words don't reassure me. If anything, they make me feel worse. 'But there's still a chance that Crowky could crawl into the tunnel wearing it, isn't there?'

'Arthur, it's a tiny chance,' says Grandad. 'It's not worth worrying about.'

'Great!' says Rose. 'In that case, can we get going?'

Grandad laughs. 'No way. You two aren't going anywhere until I've given you a bit of advice.'

'Seriously?' says Rose, but he's already pulling out an old blackboard and waving us towards the sofa.

Once we're sitting down, he finds a yellow chalk and writes 'Grandad's Top Tips' along the top of the blackboard. 'Don't worry,' he says. 'This won't take long.'

He's right. It doesn't take long, because he only has three top tips to share:

1) No running on the dragons. Ride them SENSIBLY.

2) Be home by 3pm Sunday or I'll come looking for you. (Seeing as Mum and Dad are supposed to be picking us up at four this is pretty relaxed.)

3) Don't do anything I wouldn't do!!

Number three seems to be giving us permission to do

absolutely anything we want because Grandad is a man with very poor risk-assessment skills. He once actively encouraged me to jump out of the cherry tree on to the trampoline, and he believes no hill is too steep to cycle down 'if you've got the right attitude'.

'Grandad, are you saying we can climb tall trees?' I ask.

'Yes,' he says, nodding seriously.

'Have bonfires?'

'Of course! Have as many as you like.' (Grandad loves bonfires.)

Rose sees where I'm going with this. 'Can I gallop fast on Prosecco, swim in the mermaid lagoon and go to bed whenever I like, and possibly not at all?'

'Yes, yes and YES!' Grandad laughs. 'Just don't run on the dragons. That's dangerous. Oh, there is one last rule.' Grandad selects a new red chalk and writes:

4) Avoid all unnecessary winding up of Crowky – he's unstable.

'Well obviously,' says Rose. 'Now can we go to Roar?'

'Yes!' says Grandad, and Rose is so happy that she does something totally unexpected: she throws her arms round me and gives me a hug.

CHAPTER 5

I t doesn't take us long to get ready. Grandad makes us eat some cheese and pickle sandwiches and then insists that we have a 'journey wee'. Then Rose changes into her leopard-print onesie and I do my teeth because I know it's going to be a while before I see a toothbrush again.

We meet back in Grandad's kitchen.

'Have you got the map, Arthur?' says Rose.

I pull it out of my back pocket. I've put it in one of those waterproof plastic wallets because we always get soaked in Roar. 'But this is all we're taking, right?' She nods and we start emptying our pockets into Grandad's fruit bowl. Rose puts in her phone, some hairbands and a fluffy TicTac, and I add a stubby pencil and a twenty-pence piece. We've agreed to do this so we don't leave any other 'magical keys' behind in Roar.

'Please can you give this to Win,' says Grandad, holding out a package wrapped in kitchen roll. 'It's rocky road. I told him about it when we were at his cave and he said he wanted to try some "so bad it hurt his brain".'

'Sorry, we can't take it,' I say.

But Grandad insists on tucking the package into the pocket of my jeans alongside the map. 'It's fine: totally consumable. After Win's eaten it, you can burn the kitchen roll. I promise Crowky won't be using my rocky road to get out of Roar!' Grandad chuckles at his joke, but I only manage a weak smile. 'Now are you two going to Roar or what?'

'Yes!' cries Rose, and I follow her as she bounds up the stairs two at a time. Grandad follows. The closer we get to the attic, the more my stomach squirms, and when I see the camp bed, I actually feel dizzy. Am I feeling excitement or fear? It's really hard to tell.

'Are you sure it will work?' I ask Rose, eyeing the mattress. 'It took me loads of goes to get to Roar last time.'

'Course it will work,' she says, confidently. 'Just think of Roar and you'll find your way there.'

'What about pants?' I blurt out. Suddenly, I want to delay the moment I put my head inside the bed.

'What?' says Rose.

'Well, we can't wear one pair of pants for the whole week, can we? It's disgusting!'

Rose shakes her head. 'Arthur, you do realise how bad it will look if Crowky escapes from Roar because you need clean pants?'

Grandad chuckles and draws a banner in the air. '*Arthur*

Trout's Fresh Pant Obsession Destroys Humanity! Don't worry about your under-crackers, mate. You can wash them in the waterfall. Now who's going first?'

'Me!' says Rose and then she gives Grandad a big hug before kneeling in front of the bed. We watch as she pushes her head and arms into the mattress, then starts wriggling forward. For a moment she looks like she's stuck, but after a bit more twisting she manages to pull her legs and feet up behind her. Now her body is completely hidden inside the folded mattress.

Grandad and I stand next to each other and stare at

the Rose-shaped bulge. At first nothing happens. Then the bed shudders, there's a squeak of rusty springs . . . and Rose is gone.

'Blimey,' says Grandad, circling the bed. 'I've never actually seen it happen. You must have got the shock of your life when I disappeared!'

'Something like that,' I say.

He looks at me. 'Don't you think you should get going, Arthur? I want you two to stick together in there. I don't want Rose going into Roar on her own.'

'No,' I say. 'Right. Here I go.' Only I don't go. I stand there, staring at the bed, my heart thudding.

'Come here,' says Grandad, pulling me to him.

I press my face into his slightly wheezy chest and smell coffee and his jumper. 'I think I'm scared, Grandad.'

He squeezes me tight. 'Good, because that's how some of the very best adventures start.' Then he turns me towards the bed. 'Now go and have your adventure, Arthur Trout, Master of Roar!'

Taking a deep breath, and one last look at Grandad's smiling face, I get down on my hands and knees and push my head inside the mattress.

CHAPTER 6

The damp, dusty smell of the mattress hits me first, then the dark. It's a thick, velvety darkness that wraps itself tight around me. I pull the rest of my body inside the bed until I'm curled up in a ball. Then I think about Roar.

I try to picture the mountains and Win's cave, but my mind keeps jumping back to the fact that Grandad and the attic are on the other side of the camp bed. So I focus on one thing that I've stared at for hours: Win's campfire. I picture the flames and hear the crackle and pop of burning wood. I see sparks drifting up into the dark sky. Bright orange sparks . . . Sky the colour of the deepest water . . .

And then Roar washes over me like a wave from the Bottomless Ocean. I see trees and lakes so bright they could come from a cartoon, and a river that's a rainbow ribbon. The smell is . . . sunshine . . . and woodsmoke and apples. I picture myself riding a bike through a forest, leaves snapping against my face. Cycling ahead of me is Win, his cloak flying out behind him. *Wait for me, Win*, I think. *I'm coming!* And I start to crawl.

I don't notice when the mattress becomes rock, or when I start to breathe fresh, cold air, but I do notice the light. It begins as a spot of green, and it gets bigger as I crawl towards it.

Soon I reach the trailing leaves that cover the opening of the tunnel. I'm about to stick my head through them when I realise that the ledge outside is empty.

Where's Rose? Has she gone into Roar and left me on my own? Then I have another thought . . . What if Crowky's got her? I shrink back from the opening. He's been in this tunnel before. It's how he grabbed hold of Grandad!

I hold my breath and I listen. Silence . . . then something soft brushes against my ear. A feather! I scream, smacking my head on the roof of the tunnel.

Laughter rings out, and Rose wriggles out of a small hollow in the rock. 'It's me, you idiot,' she says. 'Well, me and a feather.' She waves it in front of my face. It's black and tatty and I know who it once belonged to.

I grab it and crumple it in my fist. 'Rose, that is one of the scariest things you have ever done to me!'

'Thank you,' she says, grinning, 'but, Arthur, you're focusing on the wrong thing.'

'What do you mean?'

'We're here, in Roar!' she says, 'and I've got the

best feeling about Mitch.' Rose's voice is bursting with excitement. 'She's back. I know she is!' Her last words are drowned out by water from the On-Off Waterfall crashing past the opening of the tunnel. The leaves tremble and a fine mist drifts over us.

I smile. Rose is right. We're here, in Roar, and I'm not going to waste a second worrying about Crowky. 'Then let's go and find Mitch,' I say, and together we crawl out on to the ledge.

'That has got to be the best view in the world,' says Rose.

Late-afternoon light floods the valley and the Rainbow River slips between forests and lakes. It glows from the crystals that line its bed and leads all the way to the Bottomless Ocean which, right now, is a band of dark blue. My eyes jump greedily from the sea to the trees that hide Win's cave to the Tangled Forest where the Lost Girls used to live.

'Look at the Archie Playgo!' says Rose, pointing at the horizon. Light is gleaming on the hundreds of islands making them glow pink and orange. Rose can't take her eyes off them, and I know why. That's where Mitch lives.

'Shall we go and find Win?' I say. Rose might be desperate to go looking for Mitch, but Win lives closest to the waterfall and he'd never forgive us if we didn't see him straight away.

Rose nods, tearing her eyes away from the Archie Playgo.

'Can you remember how we climb down?' I say, looking at the rocks sticking out from the side of the cliff. They lead to the ground, only I don't know which ones are safe to step on.

'I say we jump,' says Rose, getting to her feet. 'It's the quickest way.'

'Really?' I inch forward, eyeing the drop. 'Or you could call a dragon?'

'No,' she says. 'We made this world and we put that pool there for a reason: so we could jump into it. Let's go!' Then she takes a deep breath, pinches her nose and steps calmly off the ledge.

I watch as she drops through the air, her hair flying out behind her. Rose might be moody and bossy and occasionally mean, but she's very brave. She shoots into the water, barely making a ripple, then bursts back up to the surface. She waves and shouts, 'Come on, Arthur. It's easy!' Then she swims to the side and pulls herself out.

'Rose!' I call. 'Wait for me!' But she's already wandered off into the trees.

I get to my feet and inch forward until I'm standing on the very edge. I take a nice deep breath and . . . I stay exactly where I am. I've never been good with heights, and this is a whopping big height. Dizziness sweeps through me, and I remind myself of Grandad's words: that the best

adventures start with feeling scared. My heart thuds as I hold my breath. If he's right, I'm about to have the biggest adventure of my life.

I jump.

I don't land with a neat plop like Rose. I land with an almighty splash that gives me a colossal wedgie and a stinging slap to my entire body. I tumble round and round under the water, then bob to the surface.

Rose has reappeared and watches as I clamber out. 'That was one seriously big scream,' she says. 'I thought Crowky had got you!'

'It was more a yell,' I say, shaking my head to clear the water from my ears. 'You know, from the adrenalin rush.'

'Well, get ready for another one,' she says, turning and walking into the forest. 'There's something you've got to see.'

I follow her until we reach a shadowy clearing. For a moment I can't see anything, but then my eyes adjust, and, like magic, the forest bursts into life.

Furries drop from the trees then whizz between us, their

tiny voices crying out, 'ARTHUR, ARTHUR, ROSE, ROSE!'
Then birds start singing. Well, they shriek and squawk,
and when I look up I see that the trees are full of them.
There are some yellow ones with silver beaks, but most
are bright red with black feathers around their eyes. They
look like they're wearing masks.

'Superbirds!' I say.

Rose laughs as butterflies settle on her arm. They're
bigger than the butterflies at Home and covered in velvety
fur. She strokes one with her fingertip. 'These were mine,'
she says.

So were the furries, I think as one of them divebombs
towards me and starts to burrow into my hair. Everything
in Roar began as something Rose or I loved or hated when
we were little. Usually the things we loved appeared in the
Good Side of Roar – where we are now – while the things
we hated went to the Bad Side.

I shake the furry from my hair, and Rose lifts her arms
and the butterflies take off. 'Come on,' she says, 'let's find
Win.' And we set off for Win's cave, a chattering group of
furries zooming alongside us.

CHAPTER 7

It turns out that since we were last in Roar, Win has booby-trapped his cave. Luckily for us, he's done it really badly.

I'm so keen to see Win that I run ahead of Rose, shouting out, 'Win, we're back!' As I dash across the rock outside his cave, something pulls tight across my legs, knocking me to my knees. Too late I realise I've run into a trip wire. I look up and see a bucket tip upside down. A single apple rolls out of the bucket and bounces off my head.

There is a cry from the cave and Win shoots out on a rusty bike. He does a wheelie through the embers of his fire, jumps off the bike and rugby-tackles me to the ground. 'AAAARRGHH!' he screams.

'Win, it's me, Arthur,' I say, gasping, as he squeezes me tighter and tighter. 'Stop fighting me!'

'I'm not fighting you: I'm hugging you. I really missed you, mate!'

After a final rib-crushing squeeze he jumps to his feet and throws his arms round Rose. She disappears inside his cloak. 'Rose Trout, Master of Roar!' he says. 'I thought you'd *never* come back!'

She wriggles away from him. 'It's only been two months, Win.'

'I know but last time you went away you didn't come back for more than *three years*.'

'Well we're here now,' she says, 'just like we promised.'

'And it's so good to be back,' I say, looking around. Everything about Win's cave makes me happy: the smell of the fire, the mess of toys and weapons, the wheel that's

still spinning on his rusty bike. I feel like I've come home.

'Where did you get the bike?' I say. 'I thought both the bikes were washed out to sea.'

'Well this one got washed back in again,' he says, laughing at his good luck. 'I found it on the beach last week.'

'On the beach?' says Rose, looking up. 'Did you see any mermaids down there?'

'*Loads,*' says Win. 'They were all lying around sunbathing. I was practically tripping over them.'

Rose's eyes light up. 'Did you see Mitch?'

Win shakes his head. 'No, I've not seen her anywhere. I've been to her hut a few times, but it's always deserted. Sorry, Rose.'

Rose's shoulders sag a little, but she does a determined smile. 'You haven't been to her hut today, have you? She could be arriving back this very minute!'

'Yeah, I guess so,' says Win, although he doesn't sound convinced. Then he turns his attention to his booby trap, twanging the trip wire with his foot, making the bucket tip over again. 'So what do you think of this bad boy?' he asks proudly. 'I rigged it up in case Crowky found my cave. If you'd come a couple of weeks ago, Arthur would be dead by apples right now. There were *hundreds* in there!'

I pick up the lone apple that hit me on the head. 'You ate the rest, didn't you?'

'Yep,' he says with a grin. 'Waiting, and doing an

intensive daily regime of kicks, punches and awesome magic made me hungry.'

And I have to laugh, because I'm so happy to be back in Roar looking at Win's wonky wizard's hat and wonky smile and listening to him boast.

'What do you want to do first?' asks Win. 'It's going to be dark soon, but if we're quick we could go down to the river and have a swim. Loads of tadpoles have hatched and they glow in the dark.' Suddenly his eyes light up. 'Or we could find a unicorn! There aren't many around, but if we go to the Tangled Forest we might be able to persuade one to give us a ride.'

I look beyond the forest and across Roar. The setting sun is giving everything a golden glow, and I feel giddy with the thought of all the time we've got in Roar and the amazing things we can do . . . But there is one thing stopping me from running off to hunt for tadpoles and unicorns.

'What about Crowky and his scarecrow army?' I say. 'Is it really safe to go wandering about in the dark?'

Win strides to the edge of the rock and throws his arms out wide. 'CROWKY'S GONE, MATE!' he shouts, making a furry fall out of a tree. It bounces to the ground where it stares up at us, wings trembling.

'Told you,' says Rose, giving me a smug look.

'Win, are you sure?' I say. 'Crowky's *definitely* gone?'

'No one has seen him, the *Raven* or his scarecrows

since you left,' says Win.

'But he could be hiding in the Archie Playgo,' I say. 'There are hundreds of islands out there.'

Rose does an exasperated sigh. 'Yeah, he could be, Arthur, but the important thing is, Roar is ours again so stop being such a funge and let's start enjoying ourselves.'

'What's a funge?' says Win.

'A fun sponge,' says Rose. 'Someone who sucks the fun out of a situation. Basically a funge is Arthur.'

'Yeah, stop being such a FUNGE, Arthur!' cries Win.

'I'm not a funge. I'm just sensible.'

Rose grins. 'Said the *funge*.'

And then they're both laughing at me, and even the furry seems to be laughing because it's thrown itself back on the ground and is rolling around from side to side.

'Fine, Crowky's gone.' Just saying the words out loud makes me feel good. 'Let's go to the river. We can find a unicorn tomorrow.'

'You two can do whatever you like,' says Rose. 'I'm going to Mitch's hut.'

'We'll come with you,' I say, remembering that Grandad wants us to stick together.

Rose shakes her head. 'No thanks. If Mitch is there, we're going to have loads to talk about. We won't want you two annoying us.'

'But what if something happens to you?'

Rose rolls her eyes. 'Arthur, *relax*. I'm either going to be

chatting to my best mer-friend

in the world or lying in her hammock. I'm not going to do anything dangerous.' Then she stands on the edge of the rock, puts two fingers to her lips and does a long, low whistle.

Except riding a dragon, I think.

The sound slips through the trees, and fades away. I can't hear it, but I know it's floating across Roar, and it won't stop until it finds the ears of a dragon. Perhaps even now a huge, scaly body is heaving itself to its feet and its hot heart is beating a little bit faster because it knows that Rose Trout, Master of Roar, is back.

Together, the three of us stand
on the rock, staring towards the
Bottomless Ocean.

'There!' cries Rose, pointing at a black dot on the
horizon.

The shape moves towards us, growing bigger and
bigger until we can see two huge wings silhouetted against
the orange sky.

'Bad Dragon,' whispers Rose.

She's bigger than I remember, and even from this
distance I can see smoke rolling from her gaping mouth
and her glowing eyes.

Rose turns to me and grins. She's standing tall with her shoulders back and her head held high. 'I'll probably see you tomorrow,' she says, 'or the day after.'

It's obvious that Rose is getting on that dragon and there's nothing I can do to stop her.

'Be careful,' I say, but already she's jumping off the rock and running into the forest.

Win and I watch as Bad Dragon glides closer, her mighty head swinging from side to side as she looks for Rose. Each flap of her wings sends air rushing towards us, flattening the tops of the trees. I fight the instinct to run and hide, and soon she's soaring over our heads and I'm staring at the strange sight of her belly. Her scales are paler and smoother here and fire glimmers between the cracks.

'Look out!' Win shoves me to the ground just as Bad Dragon's tail slices past my face. We huddle together, as she turns and flies back over the forest before swooping out of sight below the trees. Next there is a colossal thud that makes the rock beneath us tremble. She's landed.

Win laughs as he helps me to my feet. 'I saved your life!'

And the scary thing is, I think he might be right.

Soon Bad Dragon is lifting back up in the air and Rose is a tiny figure on her back. I shade my eyes and see Rose wave. Then Bad Dragon thrusts her wings down and they fly towards the setting sun.

'So . . .' says Win, turning to me with a grin, 'ready to swim with glow-in-the-dark tadpoles?'

CHAPTER 8

It must be past midnight when we get back to Win's cave and curl up in sleeping bags by the fire.

I'm so exhausted that I fall asleep straight away and I barely think about Rose and what she's doing on Mitch's island. But the next morning, as we're getting ready to go to the Tangled Forest, I wish that she was with us. I know that she'd love what we're about to do – go looking for unicorns – so I write her a note telling her where we're going and I leave it under a stone by the entrance to Win's cave.

If she comes back, she'll know where to find us.

Win and I walk along past the river then through a meadow. I use the map to trace our route while Win dashes ahead of me, pushing flowers out of our way and surprising furries and the odd monkey. I can't wait to see my first unicorn, but I still find myself hanging back to look at things. I breathe in the minty smell of a Roar sunflower and let a ladybird crawl over my arm. Its spots are a dazzling gold one moment, pink the next.

'Hurry up!' shouts Win, and I run to catch up with him.

'This is so different to last time,' I say.

'I know.' He shakes his head bitterly. 'No bikes.'

This morning when I told Win that there was no point taking one bike, it didn't go down well.

'No,' I say, 'I mean Roar's back to how it used to be, full of creatures and flowers, and there are no massive sinkholes to fall into.'

'Or scarecrows waiting to grab us,' adds Win.

'Exactly!'

We leave the meadow and walk in the shadow of the Tangled Forest. The trees are huge and their fat trunks tower over us. Branches twist together, forming a thick wall that seems impossible to get through.

'How do we get in?' I say, looking for a gap between the trees.

'I know a special way,' says Win. He has an excited gleam in his eye, but won't say any more. Win's always loved surprises.

As we walk alongside the forest, Win tells me what he's been up to since we left. A lot of practising 'mind-blowing' magic, it seems, and hanging out with the Lost Girls. 'Obviously Stella didn't want me to,' says Win, 'and she kept trying to get rid of me and telling me to go away, but the little ones nagged her to let me stay until she gave in.'

He explains that the Lost Girls found a boat in the caves below the Crow's Nest and used this to sail to and from the mainland until Stella discovered that she gets seasick. 'That's when they made a bridge,' he says. 'It goes all the way from the Crow's Nest to the cliffs on the Bad Side, and I helped them build it!' Proudly he pulls up the sleeve of his robes to show me a yellow loomband bracelet. 'They gave me this to say thank you. We had a ceremony and everything!'

He comes to a stop by two big rocks. We've climbed above the Tangled Forest and it sits below us, a swaying mass of green. 'We're here,' he says.

I pull out the map and try to work out where we are. There are rocks everywhere and jungly-looking trees and vines. 'I can't see this place on the map,' I say.

'That's because we never put it on there. We wanted to keep it a secret. Don't you recognise it?'

I peer between the two rocks. I can see boulders piled on top of each other and hear running water. Mist hangs in the air. Something about the sound of the water and the mist tugs at my memory. 'Is this . . . Boulders and Waterfalls?' I say.

Win smiles and nods. 'Yes *it is*, my friend!'

A shiver of excitement runs through me. Win and I used to love hanging out here because, well, there are loads of boulders and waterfalls. What's not to like? I step between the rocks and lean forward. Below me is a round pool.

Turquoise water spills into another pool directly below it, and more and more pools stretch into the distance like a chain of blue beads. They're connected by gushing waterfalls that run so fast that they've polished the rock into smooth water chutes. Sun shines through the mist and jet-black butterflies hover over the water.

Unable to contain himself, Win pushes past me, shouts, 'HEAR ME ROAR!' and leaps fully clothed into the first pool. Straight away he's caught in a current that spins him round and round before tugging him towards the next waterfall. He howls with laughter as he shoots out of sight.

I hear a splash followed by, 'COME ON, ARTHUR!'

Happiness rushes through me. Crowky is gone, Grandad is safe, and I'm about to go on the coolest waterslide in the world, and possibly ride a unicorn.

'Wait for me!' I yell and I throw myself off the rock.

CHAPTER 9

Win and I have a brilliant time slipping and sliding between the pools and jumping off rocks.

Eventually we find ourselves in a small river running towards the Tangled Forest. We pile giant leaves on top of each other to make a raft, then climb on. This is how we're carried into the Tangled Forest.

We lie back on our leaky raft. The canopy of leaves is high above us, blocking out the sun, and the only light comes from buds that burst from vines. These buds glow and flicker all around us as our raft drifts deeper into the dark forest.

'I'm glad you're back, mate,' says Win, punching me on the arm.

'Me too,' I say, punching him back, but only gently because our raft is *very* unstable.

When we get caught in a root we get out and start to walk.

We wander between the thick trunks. It's so hot that our clothes dry quickly, and we keep ourselves going by munching on the biggest blueberries I've ever seen. At least, I think they're blueberries . . . they're more purple than blue and they taste like doughnut.

'We need to be quiet now,' whispers Win. 'This is where the unicorns hang out.'

He stops in front of a line of tree trunks. At first I think they've grown close together, like the ones at the edge of the forest, but then I realise that these trees have been deliberately tied together with vines. I push a knot of ivy to one side and see words scratched into one of the trunks:

'Is this the Lost Girls camp?' I say.

Win nods and puts a finger to his lips, and I follow him to the entrance of Tree Tops. At least, it *was* the entrance to Tree Tops. Once a huge wooden door stood here, but now it's lying smashed on the ground with plants growing through the cracked wood.

It was Crowky who did this. Last time we were here Stella told us that he'd set fire to their camp and forced them to abandon it. It's only now that I'm standing here that I understand how total the destruction was.

'Horrible, isn't it?' says Win.

I nod, a painful lump forming in my chest. I can't believe we stopped visiting Roar for so long. We didn't come for three whole years and that's why Crowky was able to take over and do this to Tree Tops. We can never let him do something like this again.

Tree Tops used to be amazing. A higgledy-piggledy collection of tree houses linked by rope bridges and ladders. It was a playground in the sky. Stella's hut was best of all, of course. It was built so high in the canopy that I never went up there, but I remember watching as Rose climbed the wobbling ladder and disappeared into the leaves.

Now all that's left are the burnt skeletons of tree houses.

'It's all gone,' I say.

'Not completely,' says Win. 'I'll show you.'

He runs to a tree, finds a sooty rope ladder and starts to

climb. Soon we're pulling ourselves on to blackened planks. It's the floor of a tree house. The walls have gone, but the plank floor seems solid enough. Win drops to his stomach and I lie next to him. We peer at the ground below. 'This is the best unicorn-spotting platform in Roar,' he whispers.

We keep as still as possible, listening to insects and watching spots of light dance across the forest floor. We don't have to wait long. Soon we hear twigs snapping and leaves being pushed aside. 'Are you sure it's a unicorn?' I ask, my heart speeding up. 'I mean, how can you tell that's a unicorn and not a scarecrow?'

'Because scarecrows don't have horns,' says Win.

And just then a large blue unicorn steps out of the trees. It's got a scattering of silver spots over its coat, large milky eyes and a ridiculously shaggy mane. It's beautiful, but its horn is spectacular. It's silvery and sharp and glows as bright as the moon. I watch, hardly daring to breathe, as the unicorn bends its head and starts crunching something off the forest floor.

Still chewing, it raises its head and fixes its pale eyes on us.

'I think it knows we're here,' I whisper.

Win scoffs. 'Course he knows we're here! He would have sniffed us out from miles away. Unicorns are super-good at smelling.'

'Can we get closer?' I ask.

'We can try.'

I follow Win's lead and slowly we make our way back down the ladder to the ground. The unicorn watches us the whole time. I reach out my hand in what I hope is a friendly gesture. 'Here, unicorn,' I say, wriggling my fingers.

'He's not a cat, Arthur,' scoffs Win. 'If you want him to come closer then you'll need to give him something he likes. I'll try to find some apples.' Then Win darts off and out of the camp, leaving me alone with the very majestic and slightly scary unicorn.

Still munching, he stares at me.

'Hello,' I say, taking a step closer. 'I'm Arthur Trout.' Then, thinking it might impress him, I add, 'Master of Roar.'

It doesn't impress him. In fact, he rolls his eyes.

In case I sounded too cocky, I kneel down on the floor to show I'm subservient to him.

Then something amazing happens. The unicorn kneels down too, like he's copying me! To see if I'm right, I dip my head. The unicorn dips his head too. Slowly I get up, but the unicorn stays where he is, his nose buried in the long grass, his broad back low to the ground. Does he want me to sit on him?

Suddenly I think how brilliant it would be if Win came back and found me trotting around the camp on a unicorn . . . Also, Rose thinks she's *it* galloping across Roar on Prosecco, but what if I had a unicorn as my personal form of transport? In seconds I've imagined it all. The unicorn

and I have become friends. He's called Ronaldo and he only eats from my hand.

I step closer. Ronaldo doesn't move, so I step round his side and gently settle myself on his beautiful silky back.

'*Arthur* . . . what are you doing?!' Win has come back clutching an armful of apples. But he doesn't look impressed: he looks horrified.

Just then the unicorn swivels his head round and glares at me.

'He wanted me to ride him,' I say, wondering if this wasn't such a great idea. 'I knelt down and so did he. Then he tucked his head in and waited for me to climb on his back!'

'Are you sure he wasn't just pulling that juicy worm out of the ground?'

I draw in a sharp breath. Win's right. Hanging out of the corner of Ronaldo's mouth is a fat wriggling worm.

'I didn't know unicorns ate worms. Anyway, yesterday you said if we found one we could ride it!'

'A *female* unicorn. They're well friendly, but male unicorns are massively aggressive so if I were you, I'd get off his back right now, nice and slow.'

I nod. I don't need telling twice. The unicorn has started to growl and is giving me evils. Also, from up here I can see that his horn is very sharp indeed – kind of pointed, like a spear. I go to get off him, but, in a flash, he lets out a whinny of outrage and leaps to his feet, lifting me up in the air with him.

To stop myself from falling I grab hold of the closest solid object: his horn.

This does not go down well.

'LET GO OF HIS HORN!' screams Win as the unicorn starts bucking around the clearing. 'LET GO OF HIS HORN!'

But I can't let go of his horn. It's the only thing stopping me from being thrown off. With an enormous whinny and twist of his head, the unicorn finally tosses me off his back.

I shoot over his head and crash down on the ground. For a second stars dance in front of my eyes. I blink them away to see the unicorn bearing down on me, his horn pointing towards my chest like a spear.

'I'm sorry!' I yell, trying to scramble away from him, but the unicorn is too fast, and his horn is too long. There's no escape.

CHAPTER 10

'It could have been worse,' says Win, trying to cheer me up.

He's right. I'd have lost an eye if I hadn't twisted my head as the unicorn lunged at me. Instead he hooked my T-shirt on to the end of his horn then ran around the clearing, tossing me from side to side before hanging me on a stubby branch.

And that's where I am now, dangling a couple of metres off the ground, with Win stuck on a branch next to me. We're not sure why the unicorn decided to hang Win up too, but it might have had something to do with him rolling around and laughing until he cried.

After eating the apples Win dropped, Ronaldo trotted off into the forest without a backward glance.

We could slip out of our T-shirts and fall to the ground, but just below us are some particularly jagged pieces of burnt wood – the remnants of the Lost Girls' tool shed according to Win – and we don't want to get speared.

'Win, can you do some magic to get us down?' I say.

'Good thinking,' he says, then he squirms around until he's pulled his wand out of his pocket.

He gives it a practice swish then points it at the splinters of wood. 'Zoo fog!' he shouts. A few flakes of snow flutter from the end of his wand and settle on the ground beneath us. 'That's not right,' he mutters. 'Caribou log!'

This time he waves his wand with such enthusiasm that it slips out of his hand and falls to the floor. It lies there oozing pink goo.

'Whoops,' says Win.

'Never mind.'

For a while we just dangle and stare into the forest. 'Hey, Arthur,' says Win, breaking the silence. 'Do you remember when you massively disrespected that unicorn?'

'Yes,' I say, and we fall back into silence. If I wasn't strung up on a branch I might be enjoying this. Beyond the entrance to Tree Tops the forest is looking dark and magical. The lit-up buds flicker, strange birds call to each other and vines sway in an invisible breeze. Far away I can hear running water . . .

. . . and something else.

Twigs snapping. And footsteps.

My chest squeezes tight. 'Win . . . can you hear that?'

He listens for a moment then looks at me with big eyes and nods. Suddenly I feel very exposed dangling on this branch. 'Maybe we should try jumping down,' I say.

The footsteps have stopped, but I've got the overwhelming feeling that somewhere in the dark trees, someone or something is watching us.

'Yeah . . . maybe,' Win says.

But neither of us move. Those bits of wood below us really are very sharp. Instead we stay where we are and listen for the brush of feathers or the crackle of straw. And we look for a pair of blinking button eyes.

'There,' says Win, pointing into the gloom. 'I can see someone!'

I follow his trembling finger. He's right. Someone is standing in the shadows watching us! My legs start to shake. I'm about to wriggle out of my T-shirt when there is an explosion of movement and a black shape leaps out of the trees and hurtles towards us.

CHAPTER 11

Win and I scream and start to twist wildly from side to side, but we stop when we hear laughter.

Prosecco is standing in the clearing and sitting on his back with a massive grin on her face is Rose. She's wearing a black fluffy jacket and has a satchel slung over her shoulder.

Prosecco trots towards us and I eye him cautiously. I've had enough of hooved creatures for one day. Prosecco might not have a horn, but he has a huge amount of muscles and great big teeth that look particularly bitey right now.

'Rose, how come you're wearing some sort of Crowky disguise?' I say.

'What, this?' She plucks at the jacket. 'I borrowed some of Mitch's things. What happened to you two?'

'A unicorn is what happened to us,' I say.

'Arthur massively disrespected it,' adds Win.

After Win has told the story – slowly, and in detail –

and Rose has laughed for quite a long time, she helps us down from the tree.

Prosecco agrees to let us climb on to his back, but his generosity doesn't last long. The second we're away from the splinters of wood he shakes us to the ground with a toss of his large sparkly bottom. The tip of his tail catches me on the arm and a jolt of pain shoots through me.

'Watch it,' says Rose. 'His tail stings boys, remember?'

I nod as waves of pain radiate through my body. Win helps me stagger to my feet and I realise that if Rose is here, then she can't have found Mitch.

'No sign of her then?' I say.

Rose shakes her head then rubs Prosecco's neck. He begins a slow walk through the camp. 'But I know she's back,' she calls over her shoulder. 'I can feel it.'

I watch as Prosecco and Rose blend into the darkness and then reappear again. Shadows stretch all around us and the air is cool. I shiver. It must be getting late. 'Perhaps we should get out of here,' I say.

The others quickly agree and together we walk out of the Tangled Forest. Prosecco trots ahead of us with Rose still on his back, but there's no hope of him giving me and Win a ride. He makes this clear by accidentally on purpose flicking his tail in our direction and giving us the odd sting.

'Rose, can't you keep your horse under control?' I say after a particularly painful whip across the nose.

Flick goes Prosecco's tail, catching me on my ear.

'Don't be rude, Arthur,' says Rose, 'he's a *stallion* not a horse.'

As Win and I scramble over trees and rocks and jog to keep up with Prosecco, Rose tells us about her trip to the Archie Playgo. 'Even though Mitch wasn't there it was good hanging out at her hut. I swam in the lagoon and had a go in her hammock.'

She says this in such an off-hand way that I know she's trying to hide how upset she is not to have found Mitch waiting for her. I decide that the best thing I can do is distract her, so as we come out of the Tangled Forest I tell her all about our trip to Boulders and Waterfalls, with Win adding some wild exaggerations.

We're hot, dirty and exhausted by the time we get back to the cave. Well, Win and I are. Rose slips off Prosecco's back with the energy of someone who hasn't just walked for miles, then she starts bossing us around, making us build up the fire while she says an excessively long goodbye to Prosecco.

He gallops off into the forest, leaving the three of us to lounge around outside the cave, toasting bread and talking about how good it is to be back in Roar.

As we talk, the sun sets and Win finds us all sleeping bags. Then we lie by the fire, the flames crackling between us, watching the rainbow stars come out.

As usual, Win is the first to drop off. Across the glowing fire I notice that Rose has a wooden box on her lap. 'What's that?' I say.

'It's Mitch's tattoo kit. I found it at her hut.'

She opens the box and I get out of my sleeping bag to take a closer look. Inside are feathers and tiny bottles of ink. I take one out. It's filled with amber liquid and the label says *Bud Dust – Tangled Forest*. I swish it from side to side and see flecks of gold swirling in the light of the fire.

Like all merfolk, Mitch was covered in tattoos. I remember being at her hut and watching her dip a feather into one of these bottles then draw on her skin. The ink fizzed, smoke poured from the tip of the feather and then, somehow, the picture was permanent. I don't know if the ink was magic, or the feather. It was just one of Mitch's many secrets.

Tucked under the bottles of ink is a leather-bound book. Rose flicks through its pages. 'It's her spell book,' she says.

In green ink, Mitch has written the ingredients and instructions for making a range of spells with names like 'Whopping Big Storm', 'Frothy Waves' and 'Wet Cat Smell'. But it's not just spells that Mitch has put in this book. She's filled it with colourful drawings; fish, flowers, shells and birds are entwined across the pages in complicated designs.

We look at them one by one until we reach a picture of mountains and a waterfall. Beneath it are the words 'The End'. I guess this is the last picture in the book. 'This looks familiar,' says Rose, her fingers tracing the strange pointed lines of the waterfall. Suddenly she gasps. 'Arthur, this is one of Mitch's tattoos!'

As soon as she says this we realise that all the pictures in the book are of Mitch's tattoos, and we go back through them trying to remember where they were drawn on Mitch. 'This was on her wrist,' says Rose, pointing at a blue wave. 'And this starfish was on her shoulder . . . I think.' She turns to looks at me, worry written across her face. 'Arthur, I can't remember what Mitch's voice sounded like!'

'Scary,' I say. 'Loud.'

She smiles. 'Yeah, you're right.'

It's getting late, so Rose packs everything away then puts the box back in Mitch's bag.

I get back into my sleeping bag, and across the fire, Rose lies back and

frowns up at the sky. The smile that was there a moment ago has gone.

'We'll go back to Mitch's hut soon,' I say. 'She's got to come back some time.'

'What?' she says, looking confused, then she goes back to frowning and staring at the stars. They turn her face orange, then blue. The stars do look beautiful, and soon I find that I'm drifting off to sleep, my mind full of waterfalls and rafts and one very angry unicorn.

THE END

CHAPTER 12

I'm not sure what wakes me, but something pulls me out of my deep, heavy sleep.

For a moment I lie still, not sure where I am. Then I see green and pink stars and the glowing fire and I remember, *I'm in Roar.*

This thought should make me happy, but an uneasy feeling creeps through me. What just woke me up? I pull the sleeping bag tighter round my shoulders and glance at the trees that surround Win's cave. My eyes linger on the branches as they shift and sway in the breeze. I turn back to the fire. It's just embers now and hardly giving off any light. Beyond it I can make out the silhouettes of Rose and Win curled up in their sleeping bags . . . and something else.

Sitting between Rose and Win is a hunched shape.

Cold fear creeps through me. What *is* that?

I squint, not sure if I can trust my eyes. I've just woken up and it's a dark night . . . but the shape really looks like a person. *It must be a rock*, I think as I blink into the

60

darkness, *or maybe Win's cloak slung over a branch.*

Then I hear a faint but distinct rustle of feathers and a harsh '*Arthur...*' whispered on the night air.

I squeeze my eyes shut and wriggle down in my sleeping bag. *I must be dreaming or half asleep*, I tell myself as I lie there, listening and hardly daring to breathe. The wind brushes through the trees and the fire crackles.

'*Arthur, take me to Home!*' The gravelly whisper is louder this time and close to my ear. I'm so terrified that I can't bring myself to even peek out of the sleeping bag. Instead I bury myself further down until my head is covered, and I think happy thoughts. I think of Win and his promise to take us to see the Lost Girls, and I think of swimming in the warm water of Mitch's lagoon. I imagine every single thing we are going to do in Roar, one by one, and I don't let my mind drift for a second to voices or the shape by the fire.

And amazingly this works.

Because the next thing I know, the sun is shining down and I can hear birds singing in the trees. I sit up and stretch my stiff body. Straight away my eyes go to Rose and Win, and the space between them. There's nothing there. Not even a rock. I *did* imagine it! Relief runs through me as warm as the sunshine.

Just then Rose rolls over, yawns and opens her eyes.

'Rose, I had the weirdest dream last night,' I say.

'Other people's dreams are boring,' she mutters.

I shake my head. 'Not this one.'

But she's not listening. Instead she sits up and stares over my shoulder. 'What is *that*?' she says.

'What?' I turn to look. At first I don't know what she's talking about. Then I see it. Painted on the wall outside Win's cave, in big dripping letters:

WHAT'S IN THE BOX?

The words have an instant effect on me. My mouth goes dry and my skin prickles with fear. '*The Box . . .*' I whisper.

'I'd almost forgotten about The Box,' says Rose.

'Me too.'

Like so many things in Roar, The Box had slipped to the back of my mind. But just seeing the message brings back a jumble of unpleasant memories. I untangle myself from my sleeping bag and shake Win. 'Wake up. Something's happened!'

'What? Where?' He leaps to his feet. Then he sees the message.

The three of us approach the words as if they might leap off the wall and bite us. Up close we can see the black paint is dripping over the lumpy rock and the letters are jagged and messy.

'The Box is gone,' I say. 'Right?'

Rose nods. 'Mitch got rid of it years ago.'

'That writing was *not* there last night,' says Win, reaching up and running a finger through a drip of wet paint. 'Who wrote it?'

'Who do you think?' I say. 'Crowky.'

'No.' Rose shakes her head fiercely. 'It can't have been Crowky. He's gone. Win said so.'

'Plus, he doesn't know where my cave is,' says Win. 'If he did he'd have trashed it years ago.'

'Listen,' I say, 'I know it was Crowky because *I saw him.* He was here during the night!'

They stare at me in disbelief. 'Arthur, what are you talking about?' says Rose.

'In the middle of the night something woke me up and I saw this . . . *shape* sitting between you two.'

Rose shudders. 'How can you be sure it was Crowky and not just some, I don't know, tree shadow?'

'I heard rustling feathers, and he spoke to me. He said my name. Tree shadows don't talk, Rose!'

The two of them continue to stare at me. 'And that was it?' says Rose. 'He just said, "Arthur"?'

I think about the other thing Crowky said, *Take me to Home*, but something stops me from mentioning it. 'That was it,' I say.

Win puts a reassuring arm round my shoulder. 'What did you do then?'

'I went back to sleep.'

Rose gasps. 'Arthur, how could you possibly go back to sleep?'

'I thought I was dreaming!' I protest. 'Win said Crowky was gone. You said he was gone. I thought I was having some freaky middle-of-the-night moment, so I hid in my sleeping bag and . . . went back to sleep.'

'Nice,' says Win, nodding. 'Stealthy. That's ninja-thinking, mate. If I'm ever scared I pretend to be a rock. Works every time. So what should we do now?'

Rose drops her voice to a whisper. 'We need to get out of here. That paint is still wet. Crowky couldn't have finished writing it that long ago. He's probably hiding nearby, watching us!'

We fall silent as we look around, our eyes jumping from Win's cave to the tall trees.

'Where shall we go?' I say.

Win doesn't hesitate. 'The Crow's Nest. It's the safest place.'

He's right. The Crow's Nest is the perfect fortress: it's strong, built high on sharp rocks and surrounded by a wild sea. Plus the Lost Girls are there and they're fearless, and fearless is just what we need right now.

We leap into action.

While Rose whistles for a dragon, I pull on my trainers and Win dashes around his cave finding apples, his wand, a telescope and a hefty-looking wooden sword. He stuffs it all in a rucksack.

'Ready?' says Rose grabbing Mitch's bag. Already I can hear the distant thud of dragon wings.

'Ready,' I say.

Then we take one last look at Crowky's sinister message before jumping off the rock and running into the forest.

CHAPTER 13

Rose's dragon whistles all sound the same to me, but the dragons know who she's calling, and this time, it's Pickle and Vlad who appear in the sky.

At first they're just blobs on the horizon – one red, and one blue – but then we can make out their wings and swinging tails. I glance back at the forest and Win's cave, urging them to hurry up.

I needn't worry. The dragons are so eager to see Rose that soon they're diving towards us, and landing with a crash. Win and I step backwards, but Rose stays exactly where she is, still and calm, waiting for her dragons to come to her.

They race forward and nuzzle their snouts against her face. She strokes their necks and her touch turns them into overexcited puppies. They flop to the ground and stick out their legs so she can scratch their scaly stomachs.

Then she starts talking to them in her Obby Dobby language, making the dragons' eyes half close and licks of fire roll from their happy gaping mouths. 'Gobood boboys!' she says, 'Gobood boboys!'

'That's got to be hot,' says Win as Rose is enveloped in a cloud of smoke.

She reappears, wiping soot and sweat from her face. 'I've told them that we need to go to the Crow's Nest,' she says. 'I'll take Pickle and you two can have Vlad. Can you still remember how to fly a dragon, Arthur?'

I swallow. I want to get away from here, but right now Vlad is glaring at me through narrowed eyes. 'Yep,' I say.

'So what are you waiting for?' says Rose. 'Get on his back!'

'Come on,' says Win, pulling me forward.

We approach Vlad and try to climb his bulging side. But it's hard, like scrambling up a roasting boulder, and we keep slipping down. Eventually, I manage to grab hold of a spike and pull myself up. Win does the same.

It's much easier for Rose. She simply steps on to Pickle's dipped head, walks along his neck and settles down behind his ears. 'Lobet's gobo!' she says, and obediently Pickle stands up and starts to trot across the meadow.

'Lobet's gobo!' I say to Vlad, imitating Rose's confident voice.

Vlad stays exactly where he is.

Last time we were in Roar I discovered that all I needed to do to speak Rose's mysterious dragon language was add 'ob' before each vowel sound. Only this time it doesn't seem to be working. I try again. 'Lobet's gobo, Vlad!'

He turns to look at me. Smoke seeps from between his teeth and a rumble starts somewhere deep inside him. This means he's building up a great big bellyful of fire. I really wish he'd move his jaws away from the direction of my face. 'Gobood boboy,' I say patting his head. 'Robise.'

Still he doesn't move a muscle. He just stares at me as if he hates my guts and is really angry that his brother's got Rose on his back while he's stuck with me and Win.

'Arthur, are you sure you know what you're doing?' asks Win.

I nod. 'I've just got to show him who's boss,' I say, then I clear my throat, sit up a little taller and shout, 'Robise! ROBISE!' Vlad's rumble has reached a crescendo and my body is vibrating so much my teeth are chattering. His jaws creep open and I see fire glowing in his throat. Desperately I add, '*Plobease!*'

With a flick of his head Vlad decides to obey. He stands, huffs out some smoke, then starts to jog after his brother.

Win and I slam up and down on his hot scales. Ahead of us Pickle jumps and takes off, flying low to the ground. I squeeze my knees round Vlad and hold on tight to the spike. It's almost impossible to believe that this huge, heavy creature could ever lift up in the air, but after a few more steps, he leaps forward, stretches his wings . . . and we're off!

'We are flying a dragon!' shouts Win, followed by a loud 'WAHOOO!'

CHAPTER 14

Vlad beats his wings and we climb higher into the sky.

We're following Pickle, and as the ground drops away beneath us I fight the temptation to shut my eyes. I used to be terrified of heights – and right now we're very high indeed – but I'm flying a dragon, and it's so amazing that I don't want to miss a single second.

I lean forward, pressing myself close to Vlad, and I only loosen my grip when the two dragons level out. It's like that moment on an aeroplane when the seatbelt light pings off, and suddenly everything feels much safer. Only now do I look down at the ground.

And what I see is incredible.

Roar is spread out beneath us: the islands of the Archie Playgo, the swaying trees of the Tangled Forest, and, up ahead, the rocky mountains in the Bad Side. My shoulders relax. We're flying away from the message and Crowky, and Vlad feels steady and strong. Right now, even though I'm high in the air, I feel safe.

When we reach the Bottomless Ocean we follow the line of the coast. My face is frozen by the cold air, while my body burns from the fire raging inside Vlad's belly. He growls. Quietly at first, but it gets louder and louder until fire explodes from his mouth and flames roll past me with a sulphurous whiff.

A smile spreads across my face. This has got to be the best feeling in the world!

It's obvious that Rose feels the same way. Pickle is flying next to us, and Rose is sitting on his back and grinning. Behind me Win cackles with laughter.

As the dragons' wings fall into a rhythm, my thoughts return to The Box.

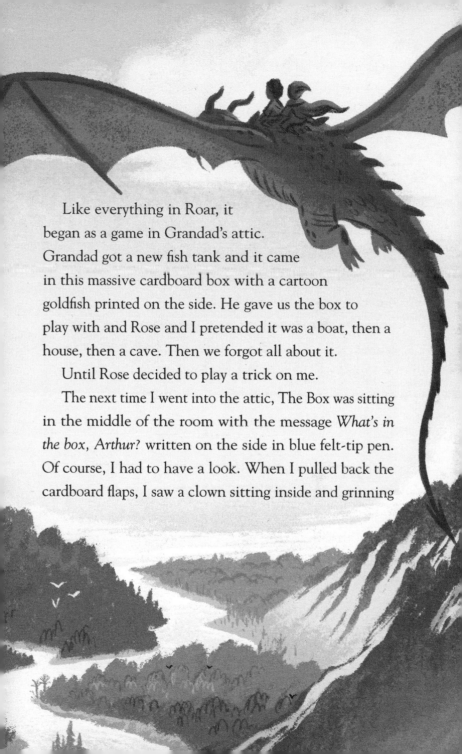

Like everything in Roar, it
began as a game in Grandad's attic.
Grandad got a new fish tank and it came
in this massive cardboard box with a cartoon
goldfish printed on the side. He gave us the box to
play with and Rose and I pretended it was a boat, then a
house, then a cave. Then we forgot all about it.

Until Rose decided to play a trick on me.

The next time I went into the attic, The Box was sitting
in the middle of the room with the message *What's in
the box, Arthur?* written on the side in blue felt-tip pen.
Of course, I had to have a look. When I pulled back the
cardboard flaps, I saw a clown sitting inside and grinning

up at me. 'Hello, ARTHUR!' it cried . . . or, rather, Rose cried.

Rose had put on a yellow curly wig and drawn a clown smile on her face with one of Nani's lipsticks. When she jumped out of The Box, I discovered she was wearing Grandad's 'smart' shoes. For some reason it was these pointed shoes that freaked me out the most. Even now, the thought of her chasing me round the attic in those clomping shoes sends a shiver down my spine.

Of course, I got my revenge. A few days later I scribbled out my name and wrote *Rose* on The Box instead. Then I hid inside dressed as her scary gymnastics teacher, Bendy Joan.

Next Rose got into The Box dressed as a ghost (a sheet with holes ripped in it).

Then I hid inside wearing Grandad's wetsuit and a skeleton mask.

It went on like this until The Box was covered in our crossed-out names and we'd run out of scary things to dress up as.

But that wasn't the end of The Box. The next time we crawled through the camp bed and into Roar, a cardboard box was sitting there waiting for us. It was big and square, and it had a jolly goldfish printed on the side.

'Arthur!' Rose's voice pulls me back to the present. Vlad and Pickle are flying so close that their wings are almost touching. 'We're nearly there!'

While I've been daydreaming we've flown into the Bad Side of Roar. Sheer cliffs have replaced the sandy beaches, waves rise out of the water and thick clouds have swept over the sun. I shiver and wonder how the Lost Girls put up with the gloominess, but then I remember that they used to live in the Tangled Forest. Perhaps they like it in the dark.

'There it is!' shouts Win, leaning past me and pointing down at the huge waves.

At first I think that the shape rising out of the sea is a lump of twisted rock. But as we fly closer, the Crow's Nest takes shape. I see twisting turrets, each topped with a tangle of branches, and stone walls studded with glowing windows. Two colossal wooden doors dominate the front of the castle.

Then I spot something new: a long drooping rope bridge runs from the jagged rocks at the base of the castle, all the way across the sea to the top of the cliffs. The bridge is huge and dips in the middle. It looks rickety, and slippery, and the last time we set foot on one of the Lost Girls' bridges we almost died, but it's got to be safer than flying the dragons into the sea cave or trying to land them on the sharp rocks.

But we do have to land them somewhere . . .

'Rose!' I shout. 'Where are we landing the dragons?'

She turns to me and grins. 'Where do you think? On the cliff!'

CHAPTER 15

And amazingly Rose and I do land two dragons on top of a cliff.

It's not elegant, and Win nearly falls off, but somehow we get Vlad and Pickle to crash down on a strip of grassy rock.

'Gobood boboy,' I say, patting Vlad's neck. 'Thobank yobou.'

He turns to me and growls a puff of smoke in my direction. Quickly I slide off his back and go to join Rose and Win at the start of the Lost Girls' bridge.

'Isn't it cool?' says Win, giving the ropes a shake. 'Remember, I built loads of this!'

Rose and I take in the uneven planks of wood and the rope handrails that stretch into the distance. I really hope Stella didn't let Win do any of the rope knotting.

'It looks good,' says Rose, giving a plank an experimental poke with her foot.

'Wait until you've seen its bounce,' says Win and then

he's off, running along the bridge, deliberately making it wobble up and down.

At first, Rose and I follow more cautiously, holding tight to the handrails and stepping from one plank to the next. But then we realise Win's right, the bridge does have a good bounce, and we start running too, taking big leaps and trying to knock each other over.

A massive jump of Rose's sends us all crashing down on to the planks.

We pick ourselves up, out of breath from laughing and running, and carry on along the bridge. And then, because I'm sure we're all thinking about it, I say, 'We need to talk about The Box.'

'The Box was fun!' says Win.

I shake my head. 'Win, you're only saying that because it was never your fear that came out.'

'It was scary *and* fun,' insists Rose, 'like a ghost train.'

I suppose I did enjoy it when Rose's name appeared on the side. Who doesn't enjoy seeing their brother or sister scared? It's brilliant! But when it was my name it was a different matter . . .

'Remember how the words showed up?' I say.

'Like magic,' says Rose.

When it first turned up in Roar, The Box looked just like the one in Grandad's attic, right down to the fat goldfish on the side, but when we stepped closer the words *What's in the box* appeared in shining, golden letters. Then there was this stomach-churning pause before *Arthur* or *Rose* was added along with a jaunty question mark.

I was always so relieved when I saw the *R* for Rose, but it if was an *A* for Arthur my chest would squeeze tight and my heart would beat like a drum as I tried to work out what could possibly be about to jump out. The worst thing about The Box was that it was clever: it knew when Rose and I were nearby, and it knew *exactly* what we were scared of.

Rose looks at me and grins. 'Hey, Arthur, remember Candyfloss?'

How could I forget Candyfloss? He was the first thing to come out of The Box, but he was nothing like Rose's clown in Grandad's attic. For one thing he was real, an actual clown with masses of curly yellow hair, face paint and a red nose. Plus, he had this creepy swooping voice and whenever he saw me he'd say, 'Hellooooo, Arthur!'

Rose bursts out laughing. 'Remember his nose? It was so big!'

'Not as big as his *feet*,' says Win.

'He used to step on me with those big feet.' My words make them laugh even more.

'Hellooooo, Arthur!' says Rose, doing an, admittedly, very good impersonation of Candyfloss.

'What about Bendy Joan?' I say. 'You didn't find her so funny, did you?'

Rose stops laughing. 'That's because she could fit in the tiniest places. I never knew when she was going to jump out at me. Have you ever had an old lady jump out of a tree and land on your back, Arthur? It's much scarier than a clown!'

'Remember the giant cat?' says Win. 'His purr was intense.'

'Urgh,' says Rose with a shudder. 'Smokey!'

And for the next few minutes, as we walk along the swaying bridge, we reminisce about all the strange and weird things that came out of The Box: the hundreds of stripy bee-spiders, Rose's tiny ghost-vampire, the gloved

77

hand that used to skitter around after me.

'How did we get rid of them all?' I say.

'I don't think we did,' says Rose. 'Didn't they just wander off into Roar when they got bored of scaring us?'

Our fears only came out of The Box if someone opened it, but the problem was, someone *always* opened it – it was just too tempting – and soon we had lots of creepy things running around Roar. But The Box really stopped being fun when Crowky became interested in it. He would sit up in a tree cackling when he heard our screams, and we realised that if he ever got hold of it, he'd have a weapon he could use against us, again and again. That's when we knew we had to get rid of it.

So we tried to destroy it. We jumped on it. We threw it in Win's bonfire. We even dropped it down the waterfall, but it was weirdly strong. Nothing could dent it. Then Rose asked Mitch to hide it for us, and that was the end of The Box . . . or so we thought.

'Do you think there's any chance Crowky could have found it?' I ask.

'No way,' says Rose firmly. 'If he'd found it, he would have opened it right there in front of the fire. He's just trying to scare us and it's worked, hasn't it? You should see your face, Arthur!'

'Um . . . You two,' says Win. He's stopped walking and is staring down at the sea. 'We should probably get a move on. The tide's coming in.'

'Why does that matter?' says Rose.

'Because soon the middle of the bridge will be under water and then it will be impossible to cross.'

I look down and realise that the sea does seem to be closer to the bridge. 'Win, why didn't you tell us?' I say.

He looks confused. 'I just did.'

I look back towards land. A thick fog has rolled across the cliffs, hiding the start of the bridge from view. 'Anyone could creep up behind us,' I say.

The three of us stand in silence as fog twists round our legs and waves break beneath us. The bridge creaks, and then Win says, 'How long do you reckon it would take Crowky to get from my cave to here?'

No one answers. Instead we all start running as fast as we possibly can along the bridge, desperate to beat the tide.

CHAPTER 16

'I think we're too late!' shouts Rose. Up ahead, water has started to wash over the middle of the bridge. It bubbles and foams between the planks, before sucking away again.

A particularly big wave breaks beneath us, sending icy water shooting over our feet. 'Come on,' I say, leading us forward. 'We can climb along the handrails if we have to.'

Soon our feet and then our ankles are under water. This slows us down, and so do the waves, but we cling

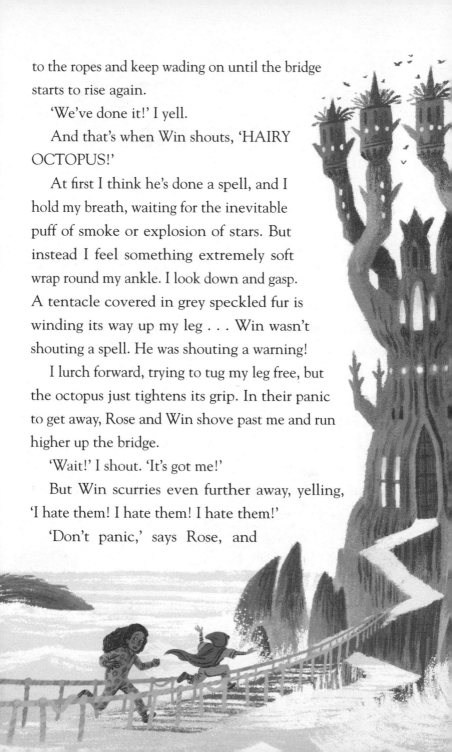

to the ropes and keep wading on until the bridge
starts to rise again.

'We've done it!' I yell.

And that's when Win shouts, 'HAIRY
OCTOPUS!'

At first I think he's done a spell, and I
hold my breath, waiting for the inevitable
puff of smoke or explosion of stars. But
instead I feel something extremely soft
wrap round my ankle. I look down and gasp.
A tentacle covered in grey speckled fur is
winding its way up my leg . . . Win wasn't
shouting a spell. He was shouting a warning!

I lurch forward, trying to tug my leg free, but
the octopus just tightens its grip. In their panic
to get away, Rose and Win shove past me and run
higher up the bridge.

'Wait!' I shout. 'It's got me!'

But Win scurries even further away, yelling,
'I hate them! I hate them! I hate them!'

'Don't panic,' says Rose, and

I honestly can't tell if she's talking to Win, or me – the person with the octopus attached to his leg.

Suddenly the octopus's huge fur-covered head slides out of the water. It stares at me with moist yellow eyes and I push my fingers underneath the tentacle, trying to loosen its grip. I can't help noticing how incredibly soft the grey fur is.

The head moves towards me. 'Do octopuses have teeth?' I shout. 'Quick, one of you, tell me!'

'Yes!' yells Win, followed by a 'No!' from Rose.

The octopus disappears under the water and I feel myself being dragged down into the sea. 'Rose . . . Win!' I cry. 'HELP ME!'

Rose wades back down the bridge and wraps her arms around my waist. 'I'll pull and you push,' she says.

I push with all my might, using my hands to try and prise the tentacle off my ankle. Suddenly the octopus loosens its grip and I yank my foot free. Rose and I scramble up the bridge, only stopping when we're high above the water next to Win.

The octopus vanishes in a rush of bubbles.

'Sorry I couldn't help, mate,' says Win, 'but I flipping hate octopuses. They're so wriggly and twisty!' He's properly scared: trembling and peering down into the water for any sign of the octopus.

I rub at my leg, then try a few tentative steps. Except for a red mark round my ankle and a racing heart, I'm OK.

'I didn't think you were this scared of anything,' I say.

Win shudders. 'I got squeezed by an octopus down at the Archie Playgo and nearly drowned. It was the furriest thing you've ever seen in your life.' We carry on along up the bridge and Win puts his arm round my shoulder. 'Sorry, mate.'

'You've already said that.'

'I know . . . but, still, I'm sorry.'

Then Rose sneaks up on Win and strokes his arm, and he screams, then falls over, then laughs. And then we're all laughing, and the bridge is shaking and it's like the whole octopus incident never happened.

CHAPTER 17

'It looks cosier than I remember,' says Rose, staring up at the tall towers of the Crow's Nest with their twinkling windows. We're close to the end of the bridge now. The fog has overtaken us and, up ahead, the Crow's Nest looks like it's floating on a cloud. The hundreds of windows dotted across the walls used to give me the creeps – it felt like Crowky could have been peering out of any one of them – but knowing the Lost Girls are inside makes the castle look almost welcoming.

The fog thins and we see a small figure sitting cross-legged at the end of the bridge.

'Who's that?' I say

The lookout,' says Win. 'She'll have a knife and if she doesn't like the look of us –' he pauses here to mime slashing the ropes, 'down we go.' Win cups his hands round his mouth and bellows, 'It's me, Wininja, and I've got Rose and Arthur Trout with me!'

The girl jumps to her feet and squints into the fog.

'*What?*' she shouts.

'I said, it's me, WININJA, and I've got ARTHUR and ROSE TROUT with me!'

'I CAN'T HEAR YOU!' she yells back. Then she pulls something out of her pocket – a penknife – and her hands become a blur of movement.

Panic rises inside me. 'What's she doing?'

'I don't know,' says Win, 'but we need to get off this bridge!'

We start running, the planks bouncing up and down beneath our feet, and we don't stop until we tumble off the bridge and on to the safety of solid land.

The Lost Girl stares at us from under a messy fringe. It's Hansini, one of the older girls. 'Hello,' she says, then she holds up a long, curling apple peel. 'Look. I did it all in one piece!'

Rose does a shaky laugh. 'We thought you were going to cut the ropes!'

She bites down on the apple and jams her penknife into her belt. 'Thought about it,' she says.

We follow Hansini up a twisting path to the castle entrance. It's Stella herself who throws open the castle's huge doors. She puts her hands on her hips and stands with her legs astride. 'Welcome!' she says with a grand air.

The rest of the Lost Girls are gathered behind her, peering at us curiously. We get some waves and a few excited cries of 'Hi, Rose! Hi, Arthur!' before Stella silences them with a look – they're ruining her dramatic moment.

Clearly moving from their muddy camp in the Tangled Forest to the Crow's Nest hasn't changed the Lost Girls at all. Their hair and clothes are just as grubby. One of them – Flora, I think – is sucking the end of a grimy, matted plait, and Nell is chewing a stick. They might be scruffy and bruised, but they're a riot of colour. Their pink T-shirts, yellow dresses and striped leggings – all patched and ripped – give the gloom of the Crow's Nest a party feel, and I think they've got even more rainbow loomband bracelets stacked up their arms. I guess Stella gave out a lot of rewards after the battle that won them the Crow's Nest.

'I s'pose you want to come in and take a look around?' says Stella.

'Yes, please,' says Win, followed by, 'Arthur just got attacked by an octopus!'

'Oh, that would have been Pearl,' says Stella. 'Don't worry about her. She was just being friendly.' Then she spins on her heel and disappears into the shadows of the castle, yelling over her shoulder, 'Shut the doors. You're letting in the cold!'

We follow Stella down a long hallway, the Lost Girls darting around us. Flaming torches line the walls and I notice Stella is wearing a new coat over her denim shorts. It's long and made of scuffed black leather.

'Is that *Crowky's* coat?' I ask.

'Yep!' She grins and gives us a twirl. 'It's a bit big,

and I had to patch up his wing holes –' she pauses here to show us two circles now filled in with flowery fabric, 'but it's warm and that's what matters because this castle is well draughty.' Then she leads us into a round chamber.

It's huge – like a cathedral – and for a moment all we can do is look around us and stare. Rose and I have never been in the castle. The closest we got last time was the dungeons. I'm not sure what I imagined the inside of the Crow's Nest would look like, but I never pictured anything like this. The ceiling rises far above us, and a curious twiggy staircase clings to the curved walls. A fire crackles in a cavernous fireplace, but it doesn't generate enough heat to take the chill off the air.

'It's kind of . . . beautiful,' says Rose, her voice echoing.

I know what she means. Torches flicker from crow-shaped sconces, and the twisting staircase seems to grow out of the wall like ivy. It's like something from a fairy tale.

Stella and the Lost Girls are obviously proud of their new home. Stella stands there, arms folded, with a satisfied smile on her face, while the Lost Girls clamber up and down the staircase, treating it like a climbing frame. 'We had to clear up loads of muck,' says Stella. 'There were feathers and bits of straw everywhere. Still, it's good to have a roof over our heads again. Getting rid of Crowky was the

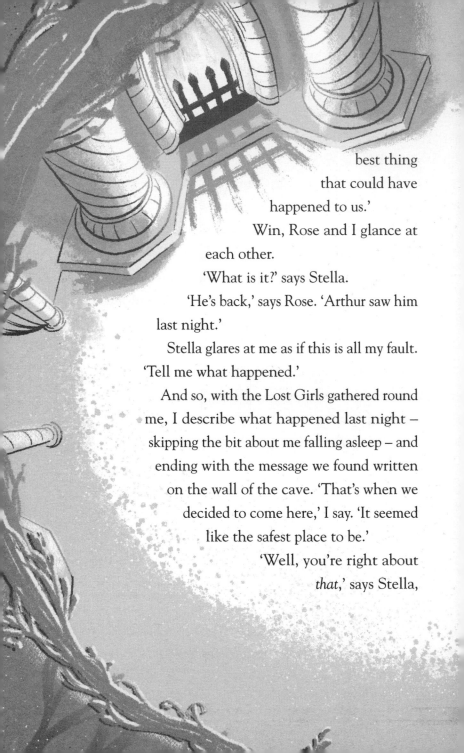

best thing
that could have
happened to us.'

Win, Rose and I glance at
each other.

'What is it?' says Stella.

'He's back,' says Rose. 'Arthur saw him
last night.'

Stella glares at me as if this is all my fault.
'Tell me what happened.'

And so, with the Lost Girls gathered round
me, I describe what happened last night –
skipping the bit about me falling asleep – and
ending with the message we found written
on the wall of the cave. 'That's when we
decided to come here,' I say. 'It seemed
like the safest place to be.'

'Well, you're right about
that,' says Stella,

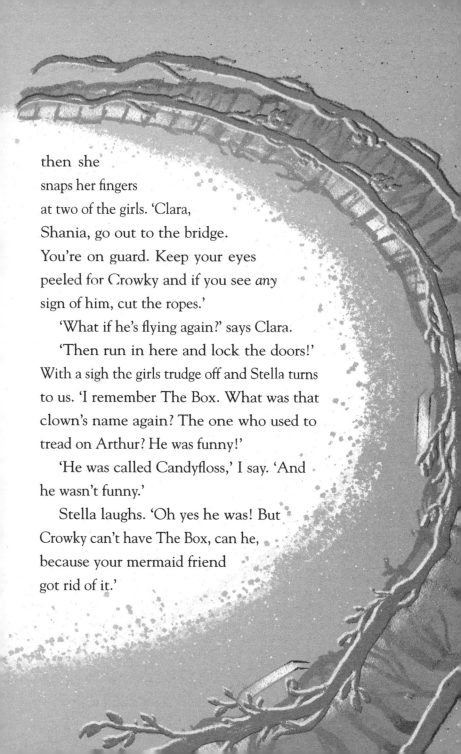

then she
snaps her fingers
at two of the girls. 'Clara,
Shania, go out to the bridge.
You're on guard. Keep your eyes
peeled for Crowky and if you see *any*
sign of him, cut the ropes.'

'What if he's flying again?' says Clara.

'Then run in here and lock the doors!'
With a sigh the girls trudge off and Stella turns
to us. 'I remember The Box. What was that
clown's name again? The one who used to
tread on Arthur? He was funny!'

'He was called Candyfloss,' I say. 'And
he wasn't funny.'

Stella laughs. 'Oh yes he was! But
Crowky can't have The Box, can he,
because your mermaid friend
got rid of it.'

'Exactly!' says Rose. 'That's what I keep trying to tell Arthur. The Box is gone and if we're going to worry about anything, it should be Crowky.'

I shake my head. 'But what if Crowky finds The Box? He'd fill Roar with things that scare us, and I don't know about you, Rose, but I'm not scared of clowns or big fluffy cats any more!'

She shakes her head as if she doesn't want to hear what I'm saying. 'It's gone, Arthur. Crowky only wrote that message to freak us out. I bet he hasn't even thought about The Box in years!'

There's a moment of silence, then the Lost Girls start giggling. 'Oh yes he has,' says Stella. 'He's crazy about The Box!' Then she grabs a torch and heads towards the staircase. 'Come on,' she says. 'There's something you need to see.'

CHAPTER 18

'How much further?' Win asks, collapsing on the twiggy staircase.

Stella peers up. 'I reckon there's six more turns to go. You get used to it pretty quickly.'

The Lost Girls are proof of this. Since we set off they've been running up the stairs ahead of us, pausing every now and then to wait for us to catch up. Right now Flora and Hannah are climbing on the banister, which is basically a collection of loosely arranged twigs. 'Is that safe?' I ask as they swing out over the huge drop.

'No,' says Stella, followed by, 'Oi, you two, that's *delicate*. Get off there before you break it!'

Win peers over the edge. 'Arthur, you've got to see this. We're so high up. It's like a cliff!'

'Not looking,' I say, keeping close to the wall. I may have got over my fear of heights, but not my fear of you'll-definitely-die-if-you-fall-down-there heights.

'See that room?' says Stella, pointing down a gloomy

passageway. 'That's where the scarecrow army lived. They didn't have beds, they had posts!' We carry on up the stairs and she nods towards a door with a large feather carved into the wood. 'And that's where Crowky made his giant crows. We've turned it into the girls' dorm.'

Crowky made his crows to spy for him and deliver messages. They look uncannily like real crows, only they're bigger and if we see them we know we're in trouble.

'Can we show them our bunk beds?' begs Audrey.

'Later,' says Stella. 'They need to see my room first.'

After three more exhausting turns of the staircase we make it to the top of the castle.

'My bedroom,' says Stella, pushing open two heavy doors. 'Otherwise known as Crowky's lair. I took all the straw out of his nest, but otherwise it's pretty much as he left it.' We step inside. Even though the room is dimly lit we can tell that it's huge and round. We must be at the top of the tallest tower.

'Girls, open the shutters,' says Stella.

'YES!' they yell, and they rush out of a door and on to a balcony.

'I don't usually let them go out there,' explains Stella, as the door slams shut behind them. 'It's really dangerous.'

The Lost Girls run around the outside of the tower, flinging open the wooden blinds as they go. Light floods into the room and what I see makes me freeze.

I'm surrounded by cardboard boxes. They're piled up everywhere. Some are plain, some have goldfish painted on their sides. The words *What's in the box?* and *Rose* and *Arthur* are written all over them. I walk between them feeling slightly sick. Rose, I notice, has gone quiet.

'We found these down in the dungeon,' says Stella. 'I got the girls to bring them up here so I could clear out Crowky's stuff.'

I wipe a layer of dust off one. 'Crowky tried to make The Box,' I say.

Win laughs. 'And he tried a *lot* of times!'

'But he didn't manage it, did he?' says Rose quickly. She flings open the lid of the nearest box. 'See? Nothing in it. Just a plain old cardboard box.'

As I wander around I realise that Rose is right: these boxes can't hurt us . . . But what if Crowky somehow finds the real thing? Looking around this room, this seems entirely possible.

Shelves line the walls and they're full of Crowky's half-completed projects. One is stacked full of scarecrow heads, and another is piled up with the featherless bodies of crows. They look like skinned clockwork birds.

At the bottom of the shelves I find a jar of button eyes. I take one out and hold it in my hand. A fold of leather forms an eyelid; Crowky's even given it tiny thread eyelashes. I use my finger to make it blink. It's ingenious.

'I hate to admit it,' I say, 'but I think Crowky is clever

enough to find The Box.'

Rose shakes her head. 'It's impossible. Only Mitch knows where it's hidden and she would never tell Crowky. She wouldn't even tell me! I asked her once, but all she'd say was: "We merfolk keep our secrets close."'

Stella snorts. "Merfolk love saying that!' She's sitting in Crowky's 'nest' making a new loomband bracelet. 'They're talking about their tattoos: they tattoo their secrets on their skin.'

Rose stares at her. 'How come I didn't know that?'

Stella shrugs. 'All merfolk are secretive, even Mitch.'

I go over to the nest. 'Stella, are you saying that Mitch could have a tattoo that shows where she hid The Box?'

'Definitely! Remember how proud she was of getting rid of it when no one else could. I bet that tattoo is on her somewhere.'

Rose pulls Mitch's book out of her satchel. 'Let's find out!' she says with a smile.

CHAPTER 19

Stella sends the Lost Girls down to their dorm, then we kneel on the floor and look through Mitch's tattoos, one by one.

We're quiet as we turn the pages, concentrating on each picture, but all we find are shells, birds and flowers. I'm just wondering if Stella was wrong about the tattoo when Rose gasps and cries, 'I think I've found it!'

She's staring at the picture we looked at last night. Like lots of Mitch's tattoos, this one is inspired by the sea. A beautiful drop of water is drawn in the centre. At the top is the moon, and below this are mountains, a waterfall and trees. But it's what's drawn below all this that's making the back of my neck tingle: there's a square box, and sitting inside this is an orange fish, its single eye marked with a cross.

'The goldfish!' yells Win.

'I think this tattoo is a map,' says Rose, gazing at the picture.

Stella frowns. 'It's a weird sort of map. I mean, Roar's filled with mountains and waterfalls. This could be anywhere.'

Rose starts to laugh. 'Not anywhere. Look.' She points at the two words written below the picture: *The End*. 'We thought this was the end of the book, but there are more pages.' To prove her point she flicks on, showing us other pictures and spells. 'Mitch was writing down *where* she hid The Box: at The End!'

Automatically, our eyes go to the windows that circle the room. Far away, beyond the miles of wild waves, we can just see the mountains of The End.

'But that's impossible,' says Win. 'No one has ever been there.'

'Mitch has,' says Rose.

We don't know what's at The End. We've never been there because it always looked too far away and, if I'm honest, too frightening. The mountains are beautiful, but they form a wall of jagged peaks we've never wanted to explore. Perhaps that's because of the things we sent there.

When something first appeared in Roar, Rose and I would decide if it should stay or go. If we liked it, we'd shout out, 'For keeps!', but if we wanted it to go away we'd yell, 'Send it to The End!' That's how we ended up being stuck with Crowky and The Box. When Rose saw how much they scared me she said they were 'for keeps', not realising that soon they'd be scaring her too. I did the same to Rose and that's why there are cats in Roar, even though Rose doesn't like them.

We both sent stuff to The End too. I got rid of Rose's fairies and she banished my ninjabread men and flying penguins. We never knew if things actually went to The End or just disappeared, but the next time we visited Roar, they'd be gone.

Win is still staring out of the window. He turns to look at us. 'We should go there and find The Box. That would be the best adventure *ever*!'

Rose laughs. 'Win, do you honestly think we should travel all the way to The End, then use Mitch's tattoo-map to find a box that we really don't want to find at all?'

'Yes,' he says.

Suddenly the picture Mitch has drawn seems dangerous because it could show Crowky where The Box is hidden. My mind goes back to the words Crowky whispered by the fire: *Take me to Home*. I'm certain that if Crowky does get his hands on The Box, and my name appears on the side, then that's what will come jumping out: something that shows Crowky the way to Home, and the way to Grandad. It's a horrible thought. I can't let it happen.

'Rose is right,' I say. 'Think about it, Win. Mitch is still missing, which means this picture – this map – is the only thing that can lead Crowky to The Box. We should get rid of it right now . . . burn it or tear it into tiny pieces!'

'You're not doing anything to it!' says Rose, and with

great care, she closes the book and puts it back in the box with the inks. 'And if we go looking for *anything* this holiday, we should go looking for Mitch!' And with that she jumps up and stomps out on to the balcony.

There's a moment of silence, and then Win says, 'I guess she misses Mitch.'

Stella shakes her head. 'I don't know why. That merwitch was always trouble.'

A bang followed by a scream echoes from somewhere below us. 'FIGHT!' yells one of the Lost Girls. And while Stella goes to sort out the fight (and Win goes to watch), I join Rose on the balcony.

CHAPTER 20

It's cold outside and very windy. I edge my way along the balcony until I reach Rose, then I sit next to her. Our backs are pressed against the tower and in front of us is a low wall. It's all that separates us from a dizzying drop. As if that wasn't bad enough, we're surrounded by crow gargoyles. They're tucked inside alcoves, their beaks hanging open in silent cries.

Suddenly Rose says, 'Mitch swam all the way to The End to hide The Box. She did that for me, Arthur, and how did I repay her? I forgot all about her and let her disappear!'

'The unicorns have come back,' I say. 'That means Mitch will come back too.'

Rose turns to look at me. 'You really think so?'

'Definitely! Remember how Roar began to mend once we started believing in it again? Now the holes have all gone, the unicorns are back and there are furries everywhere. You'll see Mitch soon.'

'You're right,' says Rose. 'She's out there somewhere. I'm sure she is.'

The door slams open and Win runs out on to the balcony. 'It's kicking off in there,' he says cheerfully. 'It began as a pillow fight, then turned into a fist fight, now it's a whole-body fight!' He plonks himself down on the wall, totally ignoring the drop behind him.

'I wish you wouldn't sit there, Win,' I say.

But he's not listening to me. His eyes are wide and he's grinning. At first I think he's excited about the fight, but then he says, 'Guys, I've had the most *imaginary* idea!'

'What is it?' says Rose, suspiciously.

'This!' From his cloak Win pulls out a piece of paper.

'Win,' I say, 'is that –'

'The map? YES, IT IS!' He holds it up and it flutters in the wind. He's torn it out of Mitch's book. 'Rose wants to find Mitch, you want The Box, and I want an adventure. So let's go to The End and then all three of us will be happy!' And that's when I see that he's written *EXPEDITION TO THE END (AND TO FIND MITCH AND THE BOX)* at the top of the page in big, bold letters.

Rose is furious. 'Win, give that to me!'

But Win jumps to his feet and holds the map out of her reach. 'I know we've never been to The End, but Mitch got there, didn't she? So why can't we? It will be *brilliant*, Rose!' In his excitement he wobbles backwards.

I jump up and grab hold of his cloak, terrified that he's

going to fall. 'Win, please get away from the edge, and stop waving that thing around!'

Just then, a strange, scraping noise comes from somewhere above us. We freeze and look up. The crow gargoyles are still staring down at us, only I'm certain that one of them has closed its gaping beak.

'Is it my imagination,' I say, 'or did one of those gargoyles just move?'

Slowly the crow blinks its beady eyes.

Win yelps. 'That's no gargoyle!'

At that moment a gust of wind swoops round the side of the tower, ruffling the crow's feathers. The wind smacks into Win and whips the map out of his hands.

I pull Win to safety as Rose lunges for the map, but she's too late. The map flies up in the air, twisting out of her reach. With an ear-piercing shriek, the crow launches itself off the stone ledge, dives towards the map and snatches it up in its claws.

Then all we can do is watch as the crow soars through the sky, stealing the map away from us.

CHAPTER 21

Shocked and silent we walk back inside the Crow's Nest.

Rose closes the door, shutting out the sound of the howling wind.

'Oh dear,' says Win.

'*Oh dear?*' I say. 'Win, *Oh dear* is what you say when you spill a drink. It's not what you say when you've just revealed the location of a terror-inducing cardboard box to your enemy!'

'Maybe,' he says. 'I mean, we don't know for certain that crow is working for Crowky, do we? It could be making a nest.' My look must show just how angry and frightened I feel because he lowers his eyes and whispers,

'Sorry, Arthur. Sorry, Rose.'

I can't quite bring myself to look at him. 'Sorry won't get the map back, will it? Now Crowky can find The Box and you know what will happen next. Our fears will come out, and I'm not scared of clowns any more, Win. I'm scared of much worse things!' I stop talking before I say something I regret. Crowky getting into Home is my fear. I don't want it to become Rose's too.

Rose puts a hand on my arm and I realise I'm shaking. 'Win didn't know that bird was there,' she says, 'and he didn't mean to let go of the map. It was an accident, Arthur. It was a dumb one, but it was still an accident.'

The fact that Rose is sticking up for Win tells me I've gone too far. I nod. 'Sorry, Win. I'm just . . . scared.'

Win, as kind as ever, gives me a big hug. 'That's all right, mate.'

We make the long journey down the staircase and find Stella and the Lost Girls gathered in the great hall. The fight is forgotten and now they're making bracelets and playing board games. This, along with the smell of buttery toast and the glowing fire, makes it a cosy scene. The only thing that ruins it are the half-completed scarecrows the girls are using as cushions.

'What's up with you?' says Stella when she sees our faces.

'Crowky's got the map,' says Rose. 'At least he will have it very soon.'

Quickly, we tell the Lost Girls what happened. When

we've finished Stella turns to Win and says, 'You're such a PEA-BRAIN, Win!'

He responds by whipping out his wand, pointing it at her face and shouting, 'Toe pipe!' A solitary moth flops from the end of his wand then starts to flutter around the room.

'What was that supposed to be?' I ask.

'A laser beam,' he says with a frown.

Next Stella sends Audrey up to the tower, instructing her to sit on the balcony and keep her eyes peeled for Crowky's 'creepy old boat'. Then she plumps up a scarecrow's stomach for us to sit on and tells us to grab some toast.

'So that's it?' says Stella. 'Crowky knows where The Box is hidden and you're just going to wait for him to find it and bring it back?'

Win looks guiltily at me. 'Well, if the crow does give Crowky the map he'll only know *roughly* where it's hidden. I mean, The End looks huge, and Mitch's map wasn't a proper map. It was more a picture. I bet we couldn't have worked it out.'

'But are we as clever as Crowky?' I say.

'Er, *yes*!' says Win. Then his eyes light up. 'Let's jump on a dragon right now and go on a Crowky hunt. We can get to him before he goes looking for The Box!'

OK, so it's a slightly mad idea, but right now I'd do anything that might stop the map from falling into

Crowky's hands. I look at Rose and say, 'At least we'd be doing something instead of sitting here and eating toast.'

'*STELLA!*' The voice comes from the very top of the castle. We look up and I see Audrey's face peering over the banister.

Stella cups her hands round her mouth. 'WHAT IS IT?'

Audrey starts running down the stairs. 'I saw it! I saw Crowky's boat!'

We all jump to our feet. 'Big black sails, tall, skinny?' shouts Stella.

'That's it!' Audrey's taking the stairs two at a time. She pauses to catch her breath.

'Is the boat sailing here?' Stella looks at us with a mixture of alarm and excitement. 'We've been expecting this. We need to lock up the dungeons, stop Crowky from getting into the castle through the sea cave!'

'No!' Audrey's cry rings out. 'It's going *away* from the castle. It's heading towards The End.'

I look at Rose. 'He knows,' I say. 'That crow flew straight to Crowky and handed him the map. He's going after The Box!' I grab her arm. 'We *have* to do something!'

A determined look flashes across her face. 'You're right. We're going to stop him.'

CHAPTER 22

While we're still running across the bridge, Rose puts her fingers to her lips and whistles. Crowky might have a boat, but we've got dragons!

And the biggest dragon of all has just appeared in the sky.

Bad Dragon races over our heads, her shadow covering us like a black cloud. She reaches the cliffs before us, lands, and, head bowed, waits patiently for us to get off the bridge and climb on to her back.

I've barely grabbed hold of a spike before Rose urges Bad Dragon to, 'Gobo, gobo!' and the huge creature is climbing to her feet and running towards the edge of the cliff. Then we're up in the sky, and rising higher and higher with each immense thrust of her wings. We glide over the sea and past the Crow's Nest.

Far below, Stella and the other Lost Girls wave to us from the balcony.

'Fobastober! FOBASTOBER!' shouts Rose and we fly

straight out to sea. Win pulls his telescope out of his bag and we take it in turns to look for any sign of the *Raven*. But we can't see anything except crashing waves.

'They could be anywhere!' shouts Rose.

'There!' Win points to the horizon where a black speck occasionally peeks above the waves. I take the telescope. The ship is tall with black leather sails. It's definitely the *Raven* and it's racing towards The End.

'Robight, fobastober!' Rose shouts. The dragon's crusty ears prick up. She points her snout at the *Raven* and shoots forward as if she's hunting it down.

I try to hold the telescope steady and keep the ship in sight. Details leap out at me: the figurehead of a crow, tarry planks, round windows, bulging leather sails. I run the telescope up an impossibly tall mast until I hit a mass of twigs: the crow's nest. Then I see a flapping coat and stick fingers looped round the mast. Someone is standing there. I hold my breath and raise the telescope even higher. A face with a stitched mouth, wild straw hair and two beady eyes stares back at me.

'It's Crowky,' I whisper.

As if he's heard me a, stitched grin spreads across his face. Suddenly his ragged wings unfold and he leaps out of the crow's nest. Like a bat he swoops and glides. Then he grabs hold of the mast, swings around it and drops to the deck, his coat billowing behind him. He throws a final look in our direction then the *Raven* slips between two waves and disappears from view.

'He was in the crow's nest,' I say. 'He was looking for us!'

Suddenly the *Raven* appears again. Win leans forward. 'Rose, we're close. Get Bad Dragon to set fire to the sails. Stop Crowky now!'

Rose shakes her head. 'I can't. There's *things* alive on that boat.' She's not just talking about Crowky. We can see the scarecrow army scurrying around the deck. They don't look broken and depleted like we thought they would. There are loads of them, too many to count, and if anything they look even bigger than before. Crowky's been busy building up his army. 'If we set fire to the boat, everything on board will be destroyed,' Rose says. 'No one, not even Crowky, could survive in the sea here. We can't do that!'

An hour ago I'd have agreed with her, but now, watching Crowky race towards The End with Mitch's tattoo, I know we've got to stop him. 'We could set fire to one of the sails. Remember when Pickle melted Grandad's chains? Get Bad Dragon to do a quick blast like that, enough to do some damage and stop them from going any further.'

I'm not sure what we'd do next. All I know is that we have to stop Crowky.

We're flying over the *Raven* now. The scarecrow crew gaze up at us. I can see their button eyes and their round, pale faces. They don't look scared or worried. If anything they look curious.

After a moment, Rose says, 'Fine. I'll do it.' Then she leans forward and talks to Bad Dragon who starts to turn, getting ready to strike. I look up. The mountains of The End are ahead of us, a fortress of rock that sparkles with ice and snow. They're still miles away, but we're closer than we've ever been before.

'Ready?' says Rose.

And that's when I notice that Rose's hair is covered in ice crystals. The heat rising from Bad Dragon's body must be disguising just how cold the air has become. I look at my hands. My fingers are stiff and pale from the cold.

'Let's do it,' I say, my teeth chattering.

'GET CROWKY!' screams Win and at that exact moment Bad Dragon makes a strange hissing, gurgling sound and her wings lock in place.

We drop towards the sea.

'What's wrong?' I shout, leaning out over Bad Dragon's immense side, trying to see if she's been injured.

'I think she's *freezing*,' says Rose. 'Feel her belly. Her fire's gone out!'

I press my hands against her scaly sides. They're chilling quickly, and I can't hear or feel the familiar rumble of fire burning inside her. Then I realise that the smoke that's always seeping from her nostrils has vanished. She plunges down through the sky. Her head is drooping now and her eyes are half closed and covered with a frosty film.

'Forget about Crowky. We've got to get back to land!' I yell.

'Gobo hobome!' Rose shouts in Bad Dragon's ear, and Win and I start rubbing her sides. I'm not sure what good we're doing. My hands are as cold as her scales. Grazes appear on my palms, but I can't feel a thing.

'Silver haze!' shouts Win, drawing his wand. 'Silver haze!'

White sparks explode from his wand and float across us. I feel a chill prickle my skin, and Bad Dragon must feel it too because she drops even lower in the sky. 'Wrong spell, Win,' I shout. 'Whatever that stuff is, it feels like extra-cold snow!'

'Gusto haze!' This time golden sparks shower over us. They're hot. They're burning. They pepper my hand with fiery dots, but they seem to work because Bad Dragon's wings suddenly unlock and creak down.

We lift a fraction.

'Goboood gobirl,' says Rose, flinging herself forward and

hugging the dragon's neck. 'Robise, robise!'

Then I notice that the spike I'm holding is warm. Colour creeps back into my fingertips and then, like an engine spluttering into life, a grumble comes from Bad Dragon's stomach.

Her wings rise and fall and as we lift up into the air she growls. Fire shoots from her mouth and a wave of white heat washes over my face and body.

Win laughs with giddy relief, but Rose and I are quiet.

Up ahead is the Crow's Nest and the safety of land, but every thrust of Bad Dragon's wings is taking us further away from Crowky and the map, and there's nothing we can do about it. If it's too cold for Bad Dragon to fly to The End, then it will definitely be too cold for Pickle and Vlad.

I look back over my shoulder. The *Raven* has already vanished from sight. Crowky has got away. And where he's going, we can't follow.

CHAPTER 23

Bad Dragon crashes down in a field close to the On-Off Waterfall, sending the three of us tumbling into long grass. She starts growling and rolling around with happiness, her wings spread wide to soak up as much heat as possible. Eventually she settles down, her face tilted towards the sun, and we thaw out by resting against her roasting side.

'Are you sure she doesn't mind?' I ask, pressing my cold, cut hands against her scales.

'It's fine,' says Rose, flopping her head back, but after a few moments she sits up. 'This feels all wrong. Crowky is getting away. We have to do something!' Since Crowky has got his hands on the map, something's changed in Rose. Now she seems as determined as me to stop him from getting The Box.

'It's too cold for the dragons to fly to The End,' I say, 'but Crowky was fine in the *Raven*. We need a boat.'

Behind my back Bad Dragon's side rises and falls.

Suddenly Win says, 'Arthur, you had three boats, remember?'

I sit up a little straighter. 'You're right,' I say, and I think back to a time, years ago, when Win and I mucked about on boats out on the Archie Playgo. 'My pirate ships. What happened to them?'

'They were boring,' says Rose. 'I sent them to The End.'

'I should have said they were for keeps,' I mutter. But Win's words get me thinking. I stand up and look beyond the meadow towards the Bottomless Ocean. The sea sparkles in the sunlight. We might not have any boats in Roar now, but that doesn't mean we can't get one . . .

'Rose,' I say, 'we need to go back to Grandad's.'

'*What?*' she says, confused.

Win is horrified. He jumps up and grabs hold of my sleeve. 'You can't go! You've only just got here, and Crowky is looking for The Box. It's the worst possible time for you to leave!'

'We'll be back before you know it,' I say, shaking him off and walking towards the On-Off Waterfall. 'Come on, Rose. We've got to hurry. We're going to have a play and make a boat!'

Rose runs to catch up with me. 'Arthur, do you honestly think we can go back to Grandad's attic, have a quick play and a boat will turn up here in Roar?'

'Why not? It used to work, didn't it?'

'Yeah, when we were five or six!'

'It's got to be worth a try,' I insist. 'Otherwise we just have to wait for Crowky to turn up with The Box. This way we might be able to find it before he does!'

'Without the picture of the tattoo?' she asks, one eyebrow raised.

'Maybe,' I say. 'You know Mitch better than anyone. Perhaps you can work out where she'd have hidden it. Please, Rose. We've got to do something!'

Win wriggles between us. 'What do you mean *you're going to have a play and make a boat?*'

I spoke without thinking: Win doesn't know that Rose and I made everything in Roar, including him. So I say the first thing that comes into my head. 'It's what our magic is called: *playing* . . . It's rare . . . It takes ages to learn.'

Win gasps. 'I did not know that you two could do *magic*! You should have told me. How does *playing* work? Wands? Spells? Potions? Oh . . . do you use unicorn hair?'

Rose and I share a look. I think we both know that the truth would be too much for Win to handle. Everything in Roar began as a game, including Win. He appeared after Grandad went to a boot fair and came back with a too-tight ninja costume that I put on and refused to take off.

'Playing mainly uses words,' says Rose carefully.

'Show me!'

'We can't,' I say. 'It only works in our grandad's attic.'

'So if you say some words in your grandad's attic, you can magic up a boat in Roar?' Win sounds sceptical.

'Sometimes we use enchanted stuff,' I say, thinking of the toys and dressing up clothes we used to love playing with.

'*Imaginary* . . . ' whispers Win. 'Can I come and watch?'

'No!' says Rose quickly. 'Playing needs total concentration. Right, Arthur?'

I nod. 'Anyway, we need you to sit on the ledge with the telescope and tell us when the boat appears.'

Win is obviously disappointed. 'OK, but if your magic works and the boat turns up, am I allowed to crawl through the tunnel to Home and tell you?'

'Yes,' says Rose. 'Just this once.'

He beams. 'Then I'll need something that belongs to you.'

In the end Rose gives Win a trainer. He cradles it in his hands as if it's a priceless jewel and promises to guard it with his life. Then he leads us up the side of the waterfall, jumping easily from rock to rock. We leave him at the entrance to the tunnel.

'Make it a good boat,' he shouts as we crawl through the leaves. 'Big and strong with a hull that can smash through ice. Oh, and put some rocky road on it and some of that salty stuff your grandad was going on about. It's brown and sticky and you spread it on toast!'

'I think he means Marmite,' I tell Rose as we crawl deeper and deeper into the tunnel.

CHAPTER 24

Going back to Grandad's feels totally wrong, but I know it's what we've got to do if we're going to get to The End.

Rose leads the way, and every now and then she shouts something over her shoulder like, 'You'd better be right about this, Arthur!' and 'If the bed stops working and we get stuck at Grandad's for the rest of half-term it will be all your fault!'

Soon the cold stone is replaced by the thin mattress of the camp bed and the next thing I know I'm crawling into Grandad's attic.

I blink into the sunlight. Rose is already over by the window. 'Grandad's car isn't here,' she says. 'I guess he's out.'

'It feels weird to be back,' I say, looking around. Less than an hour ago I was sitting on a frozen dragon plummeting towards the Bottomless Ocean, and now I'm in Grandad's attic with its new-paint smell and IKEA shelves.

'The real world sucks,' says Rose, turning away from the window. 'Let's get on with this. I want to get back to Roar.'

'So let's play!' I say, walking into the middle of the room.

Rose groans. 'Don't use the "p" word, Arthur. It sounds tragic.'

'Fine, let's . . . do some magic!'

'That's better,' says Rose, then she stands opposite me. 'You start.'

'OK . . . let's pretend we've got a boat.' I go to the sofa and jump on to it. 'Here it is! It's an awesome boat. It floats and it's, um, *blue*, and . . .' Rose is standing there, watching me. 'Well, come on, Rose, climb on board and help me explore the boat!'

She shakes her head. 'Arthur, I'm sorry. I just can't do it. You look like such a massive loser!'

I feel a wave of frustration sweep through me. I do feel a bit stupid, but I know that will go away as soon as Rose joins in. 'Of course you can do it,' I say. 'You were always much better at making stuff up than me. You made the whole Archie Playgo out of a pile of cushions!'

'I know, but I was little then!'

'Just have a go. You'll get back into it.'

'OK, OK, but remind me of the rule.'

'We can't do anything that ruins the game,' I say, 'so don't suggest anything unrealistic.'

'Ha!' says Rose. 'Like a wizard-ninja or a flying talking scarecrow?'

'You know what I mean,' I say. 'No helicopters to take us to The End or magic potions that will make Crowky disappear. There's no point. When we tried to put stuff like that in Roar it never appeared. It's got to be . . . believable.'

'OK.' Rose blows out a long breath and shakes her arms and shoulders. She walks towards me. 'I can do this. I can definitely pretend this sofa is a boat.'

I reach out my hand and with a piratical voice I say, 'Arrrh, shiver me timbers climb on board, Rose-me-lad!'

She recoils in horror. 'Why did you do that? Now I can't do it!'

I groan. 'Rose, what's the matter with you? You'll have to look stupid for, like, five minutes, and it's only in front of me. Harriet isn't here, is she? And neither are any of your other oh-so-cool friends, so stop worrying about what other people think of you for *one second* and be a bit imaginative and pretend that sofa is a boat!'

When I end my speech I see that something I said has made Rose furious. Her hands are screwed into fists and she's staring at me with a dangerous look in her eye.

'You want me to be imaginative do you, Arthur? Fine.' She grabs me by my T-shirt, pulls me off the sofa and takes my place. 'Ooooh, look at me climbing on to my SHARK-SHAPED boat. It's got a big smile –' she grins for a second – 'and ruby eyes and the flag is a massive pair of PANTS. How imaginative is *THAT*?' She drops to her knees and starts patting the sofa cushions. 'Oh, and let's not forget this sensible reinforced hull that's strong enough to cut through ice, or the chests of rocky road or the barrels of Marmite!' She jumps off the sofa bed and mimes picking up a huge barrel. Staggering back to the sofa, she shouts, 'Help me, Arthur! This Marmite is heavy!' But I don't help her because she's doing a perfectly good job of sarcastically loading her imaginary ship all by herself.

'In goes the food and the trunks of pick 'n' mix,' she says tossing them on board, 'and the casks of Fanta.' She rolls these. 'Actually –' she darts behind the sofa – 'I'd better store them below deck.' Then she gets lower and lower, pretending to climb downstairs until her head disappears completely. 'You can't see me, Arthur, but I'm still in the boat exploring and it is amazing down here! There are slides everywhere!'

Suddenly she gasps and her face reappears. 'Arthur, I've met the crew, and you won't believe it: they're a pair of honey badgers!' She jumps back on to the sofa and starts shaking hands with imaginary honey badgers. 'Hello, your name's Eric? Pleased to meet you, Eric! And you're Danny. Awesome!'

The fact that Rose is naming our crew after our two goldfish tells me she's running out of ideas. She flops back on the sofa. 'Now I'm in my hammock,' she says, 'wearing my polar bear onesie and boots made out of moon dust.' She turns to look at me. 'Is *that* imaginative enough for you, Arthur?'

I fold my arms. 'What's your boat called, Rose?'

'Boat,' she says.

'That's not very original.'

She does a smug smile. 'It's spelt B-O-W-T!'

She's being funny, I know she is, and part of me is pleased that she's not just standing there like a piece of wood, but the whole time she's been leaping about on the sofa, Crowky has been sailing closer to The End. I don't know if I should cry or laugh with frustration. 'Rose, you do realise we actually need this boat?'

She sighs deeply. 'Yeah, I know.'

'I'm going to get us some food,' I say. All her talk of pick 'n' mix and Marmite has made me hungry. 'When I get back, do you promise to play properly?'

'Yes,' she says wearily. 'I promise.'

I go downstairs, leaving Rose staring at the ceiling, worn out from being funny.

It's strange being in Grandad's house when he doesn't know we're here. It's quiet and feels incredibly safe. The coffee and toast smell is reassuring, and so is the mess. But I still can't wait to get back to Roar.

In the kitchen I write him a note – *Hi Grandad. Just came back to get some chocolate – too many apples in Roar – having an amazing time. See you on Sunday! Love Arthur* – then I grab some KitKats and go back upstairs.

Rose is still lying on the sofa, fiddling with a plastic dragon toy. She must have got it out of the toy box. '*Raaar!*'

she says, chucking it in my direction. Then she sits up, runs her hands through her hair and says, 'OK. I'm ready. Let's do this. Let's play.'

But at that moment the camp bed starts to tremble and a second later a wizard's hat pops out of the mattress followed by Win's grinning face.

'It worked!' he cries. 'You made a boat appear, and it's *amazing*. It's got a face with eyes and teeth, and you won't believe this, but the flag looks just like a giant pair of *pants*! You two . . .' For a moment he seems speechless. 'Your magic is *incredible*!'

I look at Rose. 'Oh, it wasn't my magic,' I say. 'It was all Rose's.'

Win gazes at her in admiration. 'You, Rose,' he says, 'are one powerful wizard. In fact . . . you might be a warlock!'

CHAPTER 25

Being described as a warlock and eating three KitKats puts Rose on a real high, and she insists that we crawl straight back to Roar.

Win begs to explore Grandad's house first so we give him five minutes (Rose times him on her phone) and then we search him before we let him back into the bed. To his credit he only tries to smuggle in the TV control and a packet of cheddar.

Once again Rose leads the way and we follow. I make sure Win goes in the middle so he can't slip back out again. After a tricky moment when Win insists he knows 'the perfect spell to show us where we're going' (he doesn't) we find ourselves crawling on stone. Then we're pushing our way through the leaves that mark the end of the tunnel and crawling on to the ledge.

We're back in Roar and it looks magical. It's nearly evening and the stars are just starting to appear in the sky. Birds swirl above trees as they prepare to roost, and far away a black shape bobs on the Bottomless Ocean.

'There it is,' says Win, passing Rose the telescope. 'Look at what your magic made.'

Rose holds up the telescope and laughs. 'It's even bigger than I imagined . . . I don't think the flag is *actually* a pair of pants, more pant-shaped.'

Now it's my turn to have a look. Rose's *Bowt* is dipping and rising with the waves. It's got a grinning mouth that gapes at the front, tall masts and rolled sails. The flag is being buffeted by the wind and the ship tugs at its anchor as if it's keen to get going.

'Come on,' says Win, starting to pick his way down the side of the cliff. 'Call for a dragon, Rose. We need to explore your ship.'

'*Our* ship,' I say.

'I don't know,' says Rose, 'a ship can only have one captain, and seeing as I made it, it should probably be me.'

'Aye aye, cap'n!' shouts Win, and with that, it's decided.

It's Vlad who picks us up this time, and he's surprisingly pleased to see me. Mid-flight, he even turns round to give me a lick with his crusty tongue. It's a bit like being licked by a roasting rock pool and it's so enthusiastic it almost knocks me off his back. Still, being liked by a dragon makes a refreshing change.

We land on a wide beach of wet sand and discover Stella and the Lost Girls are already there. They've made a bonfire and seem to be dancing round it, or maybe they're fighting.

Stella's standing at the water's edge, staring at the *Bowt*.

. It's moored out at sea and from here we can see its glowing red 'eyes' – actually portholes – and its strange toothy grin.

'How are we going to get out there?' I say.

'Dragons?' suggests Rose.

Shania runs up to me, grabs hold of my hand and hangs off it. 'We came to look at the shark boat and then we made a fire and now we're having a BARBECUE!' she yells, before shooting off to join the other Lost Girls now jumping over the waves.

'Crowky's gone! Crowky's gone!' shouts Hansini, spinning round and round in circles before throwing herself into the foaming sea.

For now, I think.

'What's this all about?' says Stella, nodding towards the boat.

'We discovered that it's too cold for dragons to fly to The End,' says Rose. 'They freeze.'

'So Rose made that boat with powerful magic!' cries Win.

'*Magic?*' Stella narrows her eyes. 'If I'd known you could magic stuff up I wouldn't have spent weeks building a flipping massive bridge.'

'I can't do magic in Roar,' says Rose, quickly, 'and I can only do it under very special circumstances. You know, life-and-death situations, when there's a vital need for something.'

'Huh,' says Stella, followed by 'Hang on . . . *What's that?*'

A dark shape has slipped away from the side of the *Bowt* and is moving towards us. It's a rowing boat and sitting hunched inside it, driving the oars through the water, are two furry figures.

'*That* is two honey badgers in a boat,' I say.

'Right,' says Stella, accepting this as easily as she accepted the news that Rose made a ship using magic.

'What's a honey badger?' asks Win.

The boat is getting closer. The badgers' tiny eyes gleam in the darkness and their muscles bulge. Running down their foreheads is a single fat white stripe.

'A badger who likes honey,' says Rose. 'They're cute.'

It soon becomes clear that they're not cute. When the boat is close to the shore they leap into the sea and start dragging it towards us, snarling as they go. The Lost Girls run behind Stella and Win pulls out his wooden sword. I'm fairly certain I saw honey badgers on a nature documentary once, and they were about the size of a fox, but these ones look more like bears. Stripy bears. The honey badgers don't speak. They just stand there glaring at us as the sea foams round their stubby legs.

After a moment's awkward silence Rose says, 'Hello . . . I'm your captain.'

Their heads swivel towards her and their mouths snap

open revealing vicious teeth. Then they grunt. I guess this is how they say hello.

Rose looks at me. 'So . . . do we just get in?'

'You're the captain,' I say.

The slightly smaller honey badger barks and Rose wades forward and pulls herself into the rowing boat. Win and I follow. One of the Lost Girls, Nell, tries to get in after us, but Stella yanks her back. 'Oh no you don't. You're staying right here.'

Nell wriggles in her grasp. 'But I want to go with Arthur and Rose!'

'Well, you can't. Crowky's back, and that means he's going to want his castle back too. We've got to protect the Crow's Nest.'

'Not fair!' shouts Nell, twisting and turning, but Stella just tightens her grip.

'Stella's right,' says Rose. 'We think Crowky's heading towards The End, but it could be a trick. You know what he's like. And it's not just the Crow's Nest that needs protecting; it's all of Roar.'

Her words stop Nell's struggling and she stands next to Stella and the other Lost Girls.

'Good luck!' shouts Stella as the honey badgers push us deeper into the sea then jump on board. 'Make sure you get Crowky properly this time!'

The honey badgers grab the oars and I notice that they smell powerfully like a hamster's cage. Then they start to row.

The Lost Girls wave and shout goodbye as we move out to sea. Some of them run into the water, calling out things like, 'Give Crowky a smack from me!' and 'Bring us back some snow!' but soon they are just silhouettes on the shore, the flames of their fire burning brightly behind them.

The badgers row in near silence, occasionally letting out a soft growl. Their oars dip in and out of the waves. A cool breeze runs off the sea. I turn away from the Lost Girls and look ahead to the *Bowt*.

It sits high in the water, groaning as it sways from side to side. It looks dark and shadowy and the shark's mouth adds to the air of menace. I'm starting to feel uneasy, but I tell myself this sinister boat is just what we need to face Crowky . . . and it's nothing compared to what could come out of The Box.

We pull up alongside the algae-covered planks of the hull. One of the badgers grabs hold of a rope ladder and

holds it still while the other climbs up. I watch as its round
bottom disappears over the side of the ship.

Now it's our turn.

Rose puts her hand on one of the rungs, but she looks
unsure. Her eyes go back to shore where the fire is glowing
and the Lost Girls are still playing. I understand why she's
hesitating. We don't know what is waiting for us on deck,
or at The End, or even in The Box. Climbing this ladder
is the first step into the unknown.

'Rose,' I say, 'before we left Home, Grandad told me
that feeling scared is the start of the very best adventures.'

'Grandad also says that crisps count as one of your five-a
-day,' she replies.

'That's good advice,' I say which makes her laugh. 'After
you, captain,' I add, and with a brave nod Rose starts to
climb.

CHAPTER 26

Rose has a way with animals, especially magical ones.

By the time I've climbed the ladder – slowly and carefully – and pulled myself on to the deck of the ship she has gained the respect of our crew. The two honey badgers are huddled close to her, waving their paws around and barking.

'Where's the rest of the crew?' asks Win, looking around.

'I think this *is* the crew,' I say, remembering the moment in the game when Rose shook hands with two imaginary badgers.

Rose grunts back at the badgers.

'Are you speaking *Honey Badger*?' I say.

'I think so.' She points at the smaller of the two badgers. 'This is Danny.'

'And let me guess, the other one is Eric?'

She does a sheepish smile. 'A few more honey badgers might have been a good idea.'

I look up at the masts and sails and the coils of ropes that make up the rigging. 'Perhaps.'

'Come on, Arthur,' says Win, running across the deck. 'Let's explore!'

At the front of the *Bowt* there's a raised forecastle, and at the stern I see a door that must lead to the captain's cabin.

Forecastle, stern . . . these words come back to me so easily. Thanks to Grandad I used to love pirates. I made treasure maps, read pirate books – I particularly liked ones with a supernatural twist like a skeleton crew – and I had a parrot and an eyepatch. Obviously I tried to get my pirate games into Roar, but Rose wasn't having any of it.

All these piratical thoughts come flooding back to me as Win and I run around the *Bowt*, climbing down wooden stairways, trying out the slides below deck and swinging on the hammocks. We appear back on deck wearing polar bear onesies, with our pockets stuffed full of pick 'n' mix and loads of things to tell Rose.

'I've eaten Marmite!' says Win. 'It's *so* salty and, look, we found these furry suits!'

'And boots made of moon dust,' I say, pointing at my feet.

Rose examines the padded boots with a frown. I notice that since we've been gone she's acquired a tricorn hat. 'They look like rubber,' she says.

'Moon dust,' I say stamping my foot and sending a cloud

of sparkly dust up into the air.

'When can we set sail?' asks Win. 'I reckon she's going to be fast. We might even catch up with Crowky.'

'Come into my cabin and we'll discuss the voyage,' says Rose, and she turns on her heel and strides towards the room tucked away at the stern.

For me, the captain's cabin is a dream come true. Maps and charts are spread across a carved oak table, oil lamps hang from low beams and a chest is stuffed full of what can only be described as 'treasure'. Gold goblets, furs, silver boxes and coins all spill out on to the floor, suggesting Rose has already had a good rummage.

Win starts to examine the goodies. 'Rubies,' he murmurs, followed by, 'Ooooh, a crown!'

I go to the curving window at the back of the cabin and look out. Directly below me is the sea, black and inky. The stars twinkle on the water like lights at a disco and the moon makes a glittering yellow path that leads towards The End. A hammock hangs by the window. I give it a swing and think how good it would be to fall asleep here, looking at the stars and listening to the sea lapping against the ship.

Rose taps a map that she's spread across a table. 'So, I've plotted a course to The End –'

I interrupt her. 'You've *plotted a course*? How did you do that?'

'Danny showed me how to do it. Anyway, we'll be sailing this route here –' she draws a line with her finger –

'and the good news is, it will only take a day or so.'

A day or so . . . I think about Crowky and the head start that he's already got. 'We need to leave now,' I say.

Rose grins. 'We already have left, Arthur.'

One look at the window tells me she's right. I can't see the moon any more. The ship is turning.

We go out on deck. It's clear that the honey badgers know what they're doing. They scurry around, barking out

instructions that Rose translates, and Win and I experience a bossy ten minutes of 'raise this' and 'tie that'.

Soon wind has filled the sails and we're sailing away from the land. We watch as the Lost Girls' fire becomes a dot and then disappears completely. Then our thoughts turn to food. Luckily it's not just pick 'n' mix and rocky road in the storeroom. Win finds some dried peas and onions and makes us soup. The honey badgers love it, perhaps because he puts a big swirl of honey in theirs.

After eating Win and I agree that Rose and the honey badgers will take the first watch.

Before I choose my hammock I go on deck to take one last look at the stars. I find Rose standing at the bow. She's wearing her hat and staring out to sea, her hands clasped behind her back. Already she looks remarkably captain-like.

I stand next to her and enjoy the warmth coming from the starlight. 'I thought you didn't like playing pirates,' I say to Rose.

'It definitely grows on you,' she says, then she takes off her hat and holds it in her hands. She fiddles with the gold brocade. 'You should be captain really, Arthur. You know all the right words and you went to Sea Cadets.'

'Only for three weeks,' I say. One of the boys laughed at my trainers and I never went back. 'No, I can't be captain. I don't speak Honey Badger.'

'I could translate,' Rose says. 'Honestly, I don't mind.

If you want to be captain, the job's yours.' She holds the hat out to me.

I think about her offer, about her cool hat and even cooler cabin, but I shake my head. 'No, you should definitely be captain. You're the bossiest, and I mean that in the nicest possible way.'

She laughs. 'Thanks . . . I think.' Then we lean on the railing as the ship cuts through the water. We look towards The End.

'Have you thought about what might come out of The Box?' I say, breaking the silence.

'I've tried not to, but it's impossible.'

'Maybe it will be zombie spiders or a gigantic skeleton ghost,' I say.

Rose shakes her head. 'It won't be anything like that. I'm not scared of made-up stuff any more.'

'Neither am I,' I say, thinking about Crowky's whispered words.

She looks at me closely. 'So what are you scared of?'

I badly want to tell her. It would feel so good to blurt out: *I'm scared of Crowky getting into Home and doing something terrible to Grandad*, but I can't share this thought with her. What if it becomes her fear too? So instead I say, 'I'm scared of getting hurt and stuff . . . What about you?'

Rose is so different to me – it's hard to imagine what she dreads. Except for the dark and looking stupid in front of her friends she's never really been scared of anything.

Rose turns and looks back towards Roar. She thinks for a moment, then says, 'I really hate orange slugs.'

And then I have one of those twin moments, like the ones Rose has all the time, and I know for certain that she's lying. Rose isn't scared of orange slugs any more than I'm scared of hurting myself. But she is scared of something. I can see it in her eyes.

Suddenly she jams the hat back on her head and strides across the deck. 'Time for bed, shipmate,' she calls over her shoulder, 'and that's an order!'

CHAPTER 27

The rise and fall of the ship wakes me up, and when I look out of the porthole I realise that I've slept through the whole night.

I roll out of my hammock and rush on to the deck. Cold air hits my face, and I see that we're much closer to The End. The mountains rise up on the horizon. Dark shadows stretch down their sides and their snowy peaks look like the icing on a Christmas cake. It won't be long until we reach them.

The *Bowt* lurches to one side and I grab hold of a rope to stop myself from falling. Rose and Win are at the helm fighting over who gets to steer. Eric is watching them. He shakes his striped head and scowls.

'You're making it bumpy,' says Rose. 'Let me steer!' She's wearing her hat and has a wide leather belt tied round her onesie. Tucked into the belt is what looks like a wooden cutlass.

'But it's been your go for ages,' complains Win.

I go over to join them. 'Why didn't you wake me up?'

'We didn't need to,' says Rose. 'Eric and Danny did the whole watch. It turns out honey badgers are tough.'

'Yeah, but they're rubbish at climbing,' says Win. 'They've already sent me up and down the rigging about twenty times.'

I think back to my pirate ships that were briefly in Roar. My crews were always made up of monkeys and apes, and lots of them. I mention this to Rose, but she insists that honey badgers make 'the perfect crewmates'. She seems to have forgotten that she chose them randomly and that Eric and Danny could just have easily been gerbils or seagulls.

'What can I do?' I say, rubbing my hands, eager to get stuck in. 'Shall I climb up to the crow's nest and be lookout?' I glance at the basket perched at the top of a mast. I'm determined not to let my fear of heights stop me from getting up there.

'No,' says Rose. 'You can go and clean up the galley. There's porridge all over the place.'

'That was me,' says Win with a grin. 'I hit a wave head on. Bang! Porridge and badgers everywhere!'

It turns out porridge dries hard and it takes me ages to tidy up. When I go back on deck the badgers get me climbing the rope ladders. At first I'm slow, but I soon learn that if I hold on tight and move with the swaying of the ship, I'm not going to fall. It's not long before I'm scampering around with Win, and eventually Rose sends us up to the crow's nest.

It's brilliant. We're so high up and we have a perfect view of the mountains. We take it in turns to look through Win's telescope, eat rocky road and try out our best piratical words.

'Arthur, you scabby old sea bass, I've got a terrible thirst on me,' says Win.

'Right-o me old bucko,' I say. 'I'll get the wench to send us up some grog!' Then I yell down to Rose, 'Avast ye, sister! Can ye tie a cask of Fanta to a rope?'

'No!' she shouts back, so to distract himself from his thirst Win tries out some spells instead.

'Boggle hiss!' he shouts, holding a small lump of badger poo in his hand and pointing his wand in my direction. 'BOGGLE HISS!'

Apparently this is a swapping hex and he's been trying to do it for ages. My uneaten piece of rocky road should swap place with his bit of poo, but luckily for me the spell doesn't work. Each time Win says the words our hands shake, black stars burst from our palms and then . . . nothing.

Win's getting desperate. 'BOGGLE HISS! BOGGLE HISS!' he yells, filling the crow's nest with glittering black stars. Then, with a scream of frustration, he chucks the badger poo out of the nest.

I catch a few of the floating stars. They send a hot

glow through my fingers before fizzing out. 'At least it's warming us up,' I say.

Suddenly Rose shouts up to us, 'Oi, are you two on watch or just mucking around?'

'On watch!' I reply, grabbing the telescope. Only there's very little to watch.

We're close to The End now, but all I can see is mile after mile of snow-covered mountains. I look for penguins swimming in the sea or perched on rocks, but except for the howl of the wind and the crashing of waves, there's no sign of life.

'Where's Crowky got to?' I say, peering through the telescope. It doesn't make sense. I can't see the *Raven*, but there's nowhere for a ship to hide out here.

'Arthur,' says Win, tugging on my sleeve. 'Are you sure Rose knows what she's doing?'

I lower the telescope and see that we're sailing straight towards the mountains. If we don't turn soon we'll smash into them. I lean over the crow's nest. 'Rose, turn the ship!'

'It's fine,' she calls back. 'I'm aiming for the gap!'

'The gap?' says Win. 'What gap?'

We're so close to the mountains now that I don't need the telescope. I squint into the sunlight and see that there's a narrow gap between two of the mountains, a passageway that's fractionally larger than our ship.

Win spots it too. 'Blimey . . . That's going to be a

tight squeeze.'

We're going so fast that we couldn't change direction now, even if we wanted to. 'Hold on,' I yell, as the mountains loom up on either side of us. 'We're going through!' I grab hold of the crow's nest, and Win grabs hold of me.

'What shall I do?' he says. 'Shut my eyes or open them?'

'Open them,' I say, then I breathe in as the *Bowt* sails between the mountains. Sheer walls of rock rise above us, blocking out the light. There's a scraping sound, the ship judders and a chunk of ice smashes on to the deck . . . and then we're through.

Win and I blink into bright white light. We can't quite believe what we're seeing.

'Shiver me timbers,' whispers Win. 'I guess *this* is The End . . .'

CHAPTER 28

We've sailed into an icy wonderland. Icebergs are
dotted across the sea and land is in the distance.
Black and white birds wheel overhead. They have round
tubby bodies and orange beaks. 'Look, Win,' I cry, 'flying
penguins!'

Win laughs. 'If you say so, mate.'

One of the penguins lands on the deck, trips and skids
on its stomach up to Rose. She looks up at me and grins.
'I like them now,' she shouts. 'I don't know why I sent
them here!'

As I watch the penguin waddling around the ship,
I try to remember all the other stuff Rose and I banished
to The End: the fairies and pirates, the snow foxes that
were too cunning (in my opinion) and the bald eagles that
were too beaky (in Rose's opinion). Could they really all
be here, waiting for us? It's an exciting thought, but then
I remember The Box, and the things that jumped out of
it and then disappeared – Candyfloss and great big purring

Smokey. Are they here too, hidden on one of the icebergs that we're sailing past?

Win pulls me out of my thoughts by shouting, 'Yo ho ho! Avast ye! A ship!'

I grab the telescope. There *is* a ship up ahead, but it's not the *Raven*. This one has blue sails and is smaller and tubbier.

It looks familiar, and suddenly a name comes back to me. 'It's the *Beulah*,' I say, then I run the telescope along the side of the ship until I see its name painted in swirling letters. 'It is! It's the *Beulah*!'

'What was her crew?' Win asks.

'Baboons.' Sure enough, I see a fluffy grey baboon lounging on the rigging, treating it like a hammock. My pirate ships don't seem like such a distant memory now that I'm staring at one. The *Beulah* was my 'B' ship and it has bright blue sails. I wanted to have a whole fleet of pirate ships, the entire alphabet, but because of Rose's pirate prejudice I only got to C. That was the *Connie* and she had a capuchin crew and crimson sails. Through the telescope I watch the baboon roll out of its rope hammock and swing to the top of the mast. 'I *told* Rose we needed monkeys!' I say as I watch it sitting there perfectly balanced.

For the next few minutes Win and I take it in turns to look at the *Beulah* and watch the baboon crew lolloping around the deck. I'm hoping we might catch up with them and even go on board, but a fog drifts across the sea and soon she vanishes from sight.

'Ahoy there!' shouts Rose. 'Trim the sails. There's a fearsome haar blown in!'

I peer down at her. '*What?*'

Even from up here I can see her roll her eyes. 'It's getting foggy, Arthur. Take in the sails. We need to slow down!'

'Aye, aye, cap'n!'

Soon the sails are slack and the *Bowt* is creeping slowly through the cold fog. Win and I are still in the crow's nest. Our hoods are pulled low over our heads and we're both grateful for our moon boots. The fog is thick. Win's standing close to me, but he's almost invisible in his white furry suit.

Wordlessly we pass the telescope between us, but the fog is so dense I doubt we'd spot anything until we were on top of it. This makes me nervous and thoughts of the *Titanic* and icebergs flit across my mind.

'Arthur . . .' says Win. 'Can you hear something?'

I hold my breath and listen. I pick out waves striking the hull . . . ropes snapping . . . the groaning of the ship . . . but the groaning is too loud. There's something about the creaking that doesn't match the slow pace we're moving at.

I lower the telescope and turn in a circle, trying to see into the fog that swirls around me. The groaning gets louder.

Suddenly, a dark shape looms out of the fog. The shape grows bigger and bigger, until I see masts and sails. A man o' war is bearing down on us like a beast hunting its prey.

'Ship!' I yell. 'SHIP!' Win starts to ring the warning bell, and he doesn't stop.

'What's wrong?' Rose looks up, panic written across her face.

I point desperately behind us. 'There's a massive ship! It's chasing us! What shall we do?'

Win stops ringing the bell and grabs hold of my onesie. 'It's got orange sails, Arthur, and loads of orange monkeys are watching us!'

No, those are *amber* sails. This is *Alisha*, my 'A' ship. And the monkeys glaring at us from the rigging are *orangutans*. She was the biggest and the most deadly of all my ships, and when I first made her up I wasn't that good at spelling.

'Let out the sails!' Rose shouts. 'We'll try to outrun her!'

Heart thudding, I follow Win as he climbs out of the basket and makes his way along the top yard. My cold fingers grapple with the ropes. The sail flops down and the honey badgers pull it tight. I slip and slide to the next sail and tug at a tricky knot. But it's no good. The *Alisha* is already alongside us.

Clinging to a rope, I watch as grappling hooks are thrown across the gap, followed by a net. Now our ships are locked together. Next come the orangutans. They bound easily across the net then spread over the deck of the *Bowt*.

'They are *fast*,' says Win, his voice filled with admiration.

145

A scream rips through the air and we turn in time to see an orangutan flying towards us, teeth bared. I scurry sideways, but a long muscly arm reaches for me, a hand clamps down on my shoulder and I'm yanked back. There's no escape. The orangutan tucks Win and me under the same smelly armpit then goes back towards the *Alisha*, swinging from rope to rope.

'Arthur, I know this hurts –' Win says, his elbow pressed into my face – 'but *this* is what it feels like to be a monkey. Here comes the big one!' Our captor is picking up speed, getting ready to leap from our ship back to the *Alisha*. Below us, Rose and the honey badgers are being forced across the net by kicking, prodding

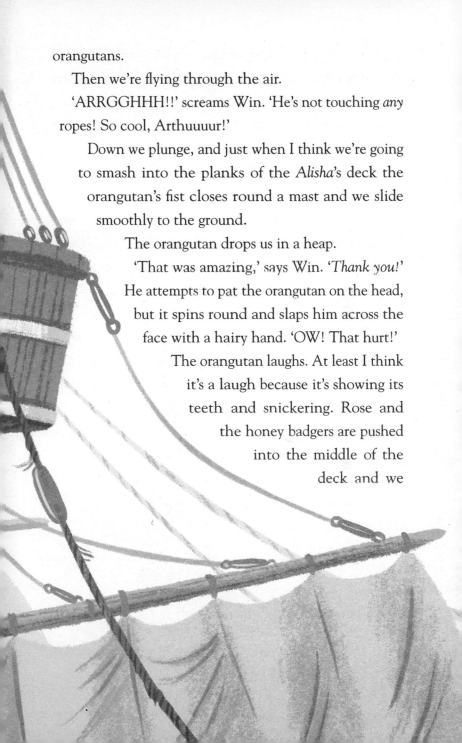

orangutans.

Then we're flying through the air.

'ARRGGHHH!!' screams Win. 'He's not touching *any* ropes! So cool, Arthuuuur!'

Down we plunge, and just when I think we're going to smash into the planks of the *Alisha*'s deck the orangutan's fist closes round a mast and we slide smoothly to the ground.

The orangutan drops us in a heap.

'That was amazing,' says Win. '*Thank you!*'

He attempts to pat the orangutan on the head, but it spins round and slaps him across the face with a hairy hand. 'OW! That hurt!'

The orangutan laughs. At least I think it's a laugh because it's showing its teeth and snickering. Rose and the honey badgers are pushed into the middle of the deck and we gather in a huddle.

'We didn't stand a chance,' I say, rubbing my stomach where the orangutan squeezed me. 'They were so fast!'

Rose holds out her hand and I see a semi-circle of red marks. 'One bit me,' she says, her voice wobbling. 'I didn't fight back, or anything, and it still bit me. I told you pirates were bad news, Arthur!'

The orangutans are circling us, snarling at Danny and Eric, who in turn are baring their teeth and snarling back. Suddenly I realise that the sounds aren't random acts of aggression. The animals are talking to each other, or rather yelling at each other.

'Rose, can you understand what they're saying?'

She frowns, trying to pick out a word from the babble of screams and barks. 'The orangutans are saying stuff like *our captain's crazy . . . you're going to be chucked in the sea for the sharks to eat . . .*'

'*What?!*' says Win.

'Shh!' says Rose, straining to hear. 'That big one just said, *Captain's going to cut you into little pieces and make you into sushi . . . no, stew.*'

'I don't want to be stew!' says Win, his eyes wide with panic. 'What's stew?'

'It's like thick soup,' I say.

Win yelps and the orangutans turn in our direction and start to creep closer, their eyes gleaming. The five of us squeeze together, a mass of black-and-white fur and trembling bodies.

'Arthur, can't you do something?' says Rose. 'You're the one who *loves* pirates so much!'

'Tell them who we are,' I say, thinking fast. 'Tell them that we're the Masters of Roar and I'm their, um –' I try to think of the best word, one that suggests ultimate piratical power – 'I'm their *Sea Lord*, and I'm taking command of this ship.'

Rose does her best to translate my words into Ape and finishes her speech by pointing at me.

For a moment there is silence – a respectful silence, I think – until the orangutans start growling and laughing at the same time. One of them manages to get it together enough to shout some words in Rose's face.

'What did it say?' I ask.

Rose looks at me with big eyes. 'It said, *Sea Lord is the main ingredient of the captain's stew . . . yum, yum.*'

'It actually said, "yum, yum"?'

Rose nods and Win puts an arm round my shoulder. 'Bad luck, shipmate.'

CHAPTER 29

Arms yanked behind our backs, Win, Rose and I are pushed towards the captain's cabin.

My legs feel wobbly as I start to wonder what sort of person, or ape, lies behind those elaborately carved doors. I frantically search my memory for any cannibalistic stew-loving captains that were in my pirate games. Unfortunately it sounds like exactly the sort of thing I would have made up.

I hear a snarl, a hand hits me on the flat of my back and I stumble forward.

'I think you're supposed to open the door, Arthur,' says Rose.

I reach for the handle, take a deep breath and turn. It swings open and we're shoved inside a shadowy room. The door bangs shut, leaving us in darkness.

There are no lamps, and shutters cover the windows. But that doesn't mean there's no light. Strange glowing lights are dotted everywhere. I see worms, starfish, pulsing fluorescent flower buds, and they are all trapped inside jars.

'*What is this place?*' whispers Rose.

It's not just the jars that are strange. The air is tinged with the smell of burning herbs and dank water. In fact, I can hear a *drip, drip, drip* coming from in front of us and, even more alarming, the swish of something large moving through water.

There's a splash, the flare of a match, and a lamp is lit at the back of the cabin.

And then . . . I can't quite believe what I'm seeing.

Brown eyes stare at us from a brown face. I see strong arms, a ferocious scowl, webbed fingers, a mass of knotted blue hair and lots and lots of tattoos.

'*Mitch?*' whispers Rose.

Mitch is sitting on the edge of a giant copper bath, her tail trailing in the water. Recognition flashes across her face. 'ROSE TROUT!' she bellows, then she lifts her tail and slams it down, showering us with water.

With a cry of joy Rose shoves past me, and throws herself at her long-lost friend.

Mitch pulls her into a tight hug. 'Is that really you, Rose? I don't believe it!'

Then a lot of things happen at once. Mitch yanks a rope, opening a shutter, Rose laughs with happiness and Win slips over in a pool of water, pulling me down with him.

When we get to our feet, Mitch's arms are still wrapped

tight round Rose. In fact, she looks like she's never going to let go. Rose meanwhile is staring at Mitch with a mixture of wonder and pure happiness. I realise I haven't seen Rose smile like this in ages. It's totally different to her selfie smile, or her school smile. It's massive, beaming, and it takes over her whole face.

Mitch does a hearty cackle. 'Sorry about my crew and the creepy room and what-not. I try to be a bit lairy when we take prisoners, you know, show them who's boss. Well, I'm sorry for *you*, Rose. Win and Arthur –' she waggles a webbed finger in our direction – 'not so much. HA HA HA!'

Hearing that laugh again, deep-bellied and gravelly, I realise just how suited Mitch is to life as a pirate captain.

Mitch holds Rose away from her and looks at her appraisingly. 'You've changed,' she says. 'Got bigger and stuff . . . Why aren't you talking?'

'Because I'm . . . happy,' manages Rose. 'I missed you.'

'Yeah, I missed you too,' says Mitch. Then she grins, swings her tail out of the tub and uses it to tap a battered leather sofa. 'Grab a pew, me hearties, and tell me where you've been, and why you're sailing around in some weird shark ship dressed as polar bears.'

The three of us perch in a row and Win and I take it in turns to talk, explaining how Crowky left us a message and that this led us to finding the map – her tattoo – and then the crow stealing it. Rose just stares at Mitch as if she might disappear at any moment.

'We *can't* let him get The Box,' I say. 'Me and Rose, our fears are different now. We don't know what would come out of it, but it would definitely be much worse than a clown with big feet!'

'Hold up,' says Mitch. 'Explain that bit about my tattoo again.'

'One of your tattoos shows where you hid The Box,' I say. 'We know because we found a copy of it in your book.' Rose gets the tattoo kit out of the satchel and hands Mitch her book. She starts flicking through it. 'You won't find it

in there,' I add, making Win shift uncomfortably. 'It . . .
fell out and Crowky got his hands on it.'

'And that is why it's so brilliant that we've found you,'
says Rose, finally finding her voice. 'The picture showed
mountains and a big waterfall, but it's not a proper map.
Crowky will be desperately trying to work out where he's
supposed to go, but you can lead us straight there!'

Mitch stares at us with a confused look on her face.
'I'm sorry, but I do not know *what* you are talking about.'

'The map is one of your tattoos,' I say as slowly and
clearly as possible, wondering why Mitch is finding this
so hard to understand.

'What did it look like?' she says.

'A big drop of water,' says Rose, 'with loads of stuff
inside it, and, right at the bottom there was this little box
and a goldfish.'

'Yep, that's one of mine,' Mitch says, pushing up the
sleeve of her black shirt and pointing at a tattoo on the
inside of her left wrist.

Relief rushes through me, 'It's the same!' I say. 'Look,
the fish's eye is a cross and the moon is bright yellow.
They're identical.'

'We worked out that you hid The Box at The End,' says
Rose, 'but that's as far as we got. Mitch, where exactly did
you hide The Box?'

Mitch laughs and slaps Rose on the shoulder. 'I haven't
got a clue, Rose, me old mucker!'

CHAPTER 30

Silence fills the cabin. Rose and I share a look of worry.
'I don't know what *any* of my tattoos mean!' Mitch
says cheerfully. Then she rolls back into the bath and
wriggles around a bit. She pulls herself out and flops on
the sofa next to Rose. 'Sorry, itchy tail,' she says, flinging
her mass of wet hair over our shoulders.

'But . . . Mitch,' says Rose, 'you drew every single one
of your tattoos for a reason, an *important* reason. That one
there –' she points at a black feather crossed with a rosebud
– 'you put that on your wrist after Crowky and I had a fight
in the waterfall. He stole your spell book, but I got it back!'

'You're probably right.' Mitch presses her finger against
the little box with the fish in it. 'And I'm sure this is a map
that shows where I hid The Box, but that's what I keep
trying to tell you: *I can't remember*. My memory's gone.
Well, lots of it. I'm surprised I even remember you three.'

And just like that, our joy at finding Mitch and knowing
we are so close to getting The Box fades away.

Mitch doesn't seem to notice the effect her words have on us. She pulls up her other sleeve and turns her arms from side to side, examining her tattoos. Cheerfully she starts to point them out, one by one. 'What's that? A rat or a mouse? I don't know! And what's with all these starfish? There are loads of them. I've got some fish here and bubbles, tons of them, and something that looks like a weasel – actually, Win, that might be a picture of you – HA HA! I must have known what they meant once, but now they're just a load of random pictures.' She ends her speech with a smile and a shrug.

'How did you lose your memory?' asks Rose. She's shrunk low on the sofa. I'm not sure she wants to hear this story.

'It's so strange. One day I was lying in my hammock chatting to a mermaid and the next thing I knew – bang! – I was floating in the Bottomless Ocean, only I didn't know how I had got there.' Mitch laughs in amazement, but Rose and I know *exactly* how she got there. As we grew up and began to forget about Roar, things started to disappear. The moment Mitch vanished must have been the moment when Rose's belief in her finally faded away.

'But you were fine, right?' I say, knowing how bad Rose must be feeling right now. 'No lasting damage?'

Mitch snorts. 'Well, my tail was still there, and my hair was looking as awesome as ever, but I'd lost my memory. I knew that I was an uber-powerful mer-witch, and I could remember some people, like you three, and Crowky, but that was about it.'

'So what did you do?' asks Rose.

Mitch shrugs. 'I swam, and the water got colder and colder, and that's when the crew of the *Alisha* fished me out of the sea in a net. At first they were going to chuck me back in – they were annoyed I wasn't something they could eat – but with a little bit of persuasion –' she pauses here to grin – 'and quite a lot of magic, they decided to make me their captain.'

'So you didn't forget your magic?' asks Win. He almost sounds disappointed as he says this, and I remember how jealous he used to be of Mitch's skills.

'I forgot a bit,' says Mitch, 'but it came back pretty fast.' Then she leans back, grabs a jar off a shelf, takes out a pinch of what look like petals and blows them into the air. She mutters something under her breath and instantly they turn into burning lights that float about the cabin.

They twist and turn, revealing shelf after shelf of bottles and jars, all stuffed full of ingredients. Blobs of seaweed pulsate and glow. Worms squirm round each other. Leaves, petals, feathers, pieces of fur, stones, crystals and things I just can't identify are packed into each container. I read some of the labels: *Petrel Chick Feathers, Penguin Breath: HOT, Penguin Breath: TEPID, Seal Droppings, Rain, Mist, Mangy Rabbit* . . .

Rose smiles as the flickers of light continue their journey around the room, revealing dried objects hanging from the ceiling: bunches of herbs, garlands of mushrooms, and some furry things that look worryingly like tails.

'Still don't use a wand?' says Win, casually taking out his own wand and muttering: 'Fuzz button.' A slight wind wafts through the cabin. He nods. 'Just what I wanted to happen.'

Mitch snorts. 'A *wand*? I don't think so, Win. I do proper magic, not party tricks like you. I respect the laws of M.O.O.N. and as a consequence my magic is powerful and profound.'

Win tries to do his own mocking snort. 'M.O.O.N. That's just herb tea and mushed-up flowers to put on burns!'

'What *is* M.O.O.N.?' I ask.

Mitch curls her fingers into a fist. The letters M.O.O.N. are tattooed on her knuckles. 'M – I can *make*, but I can't break,' she says. 'That means I can't blow stuff up. O – *Owls* are sacred. I can never harm them. The next O stands for *Ooooooh!* That's what my magic has to make you feel. So I can't use magic because I'm feeling lazy, like to make a cup of tea.' She waggles her fist around. 'Finally, N – *nature*. I can only use what nature *provides* to make a spell, and my spell has to be *part* of nature.'

'So, you could use the sun, but you couldn't use . . . my trainers?' I say.

'Exactly, Arthur.' Then she shoots an annoying smile in Win's direction. 'M.O.O.N., the most noble and best form of magic *EVER*!'

And also something that was obviously made up by my sister when she was about six.

'It sounds rubbish,' mutters Win.

'Well, it works for me.' Mitch grabs a handful of dried seaweed, puts it on the tip of her tail and gently bats it towards Win's face.

Instantly the seaweed vanishes and the cabin window blows open. Then there is a *swoosh* and a rogue wave arcs through the window and hits Win in the face, totally soaking him.

'HA HA!' cackles Mitch, collapsing against Rose, who is also shaking with laughter.

Obviously I feel bad for my wet friend, but it's so good to see Rose laughing again, and I mean proper belly laughing, that I can't help joining in.

Perhaps it's this that makes Win draw his wand and yell, 'FLOATY POTATO!' A single green star bursts from his wand, lands on his knee and stings him. 'OW!' He rubs hard at the spot. 'I must have got the words wrong. There should have been at least five of them, and they should have landed all over Mitch!'

Mitch has recovered enough to throw a pile of blue feathers in the air. In a flash they turn to snow – blue snow – which falls directly over Win.

'Whistle fur!' he cries. This is Win's best spell – his marshmallow spell – and he says it with plenty of passion and conviction because marshmallows start pinging out of his wand like it's a marshmallow machine gun.

WHACK! Mitch sends some crushed beetles towards Win that become a whirl of sand.

'Jazzy cheese!' Smelly green smoke billows from Win's wand.

And so it goes on, and Rose and I find ourselves caught in the crossfire of a magic-off. Mitch is obviously the winner – her pink hailstones are truly magnificent – but this doesn't stop Win from magicking up endless smoke and stars until we're all choking and wet and struggling to breathe.

'Watch this,' says an out-of-breath Mitch, pouring a ladle of something green and luminous on her tail, but we don't get to see her next spell because we're interrupted by a gentle *tap*, *tap*, *tap*, coming from the window.

Something is sitting there. A crow.

It has a curved beak and two huge yellow eyes. It leans forward and pecks the window again. *Tap, tap, tap.* When it sees that it's got our attention it does something extremely creepy. It lifts up its wing, curves its feathers and waves. Just like a person.

'Urgh,' says Mitch. 'What is *that* thing?'

'It's one of Crowky's birds,' says Rose. 'He makes them . . . somehow. They're his spies –'

'And messengers,' I add.

'Right.' Mitch leaps into action, reaching up and snatching a bottle of deep blue powder off the shelf. 'Let's send a message to Crowky.'

But before she can even unscrew the lid, the crow has nudged the window open with its beak and dived into the cabin. Its huge wings knock the bottle from Mitch's hands, then it swoops around the room, once, twice, shrieking as it goes. I throw my arms up to protect my head and its claws graze my skin. Bottles smash and dried mushrooms rain down on us.

Then, as quickly as it arrived, the crow flies out of the window and back across the icy sea.

We take in the destruction in the room. The crow has done considerable damage, smashing a whole row of bottles and scattering their contents over the floor. Next to my feet some little fish wriggle in a puddle of sparkly liquid.

Then I see a folded piece of paper has been dropped in my lap. 'Look,' I say. When I open it I find four words scrawled inside: *WHAT'S IN THE BOX?*

'Do you think he's found it?' Rose's voice is quiet. I can tell how scared she is.

Mitch notices Rose's fear too. She slams her tail down and lets out a growl of rage. It's so scary I shrink back against Win. Then she jabs a finger at the tattoo on her wrist and says, 'We are going to find The Box before that stupid scarecrow can get his hands on it because I do not like it when people mess with my magic, and I *hate it* when they MESS WITH MY FRIENDS!'

Then she scoops up some of the spilled ingredients and slaps them on her tail. She pulls herself over to the window and flings the whole lot out. We hear a rumble of thunder, quiet at first then building in intensity. Next comes a flash of lightning that's so colossal it jolts my heart and seems to split the sky in two.

'TAKE THAT, CROWKY!' she screams out of the window.

CHAPTER 31

'Hot tub, anyone?' Despite having just made a storm, Mitch's voice is unnervingly calm.

Without waiting for an answer she reaches up and pulls herself through a hatch in the ceiling. We go outside and find her swimming round a circular pool overlooking the deck. The pool is similar to her bath, only bigger, and steam rises from the water. She rests on the copper side and pulls up her sleeve. 'Right, let's work out where I hid The Box.'

Her tail flips from side to side as she stares at the tattoo. We all hold our breath.

After a moment she points at the waterfall. 'I think I know where this is. There's this waterfall that we call the Vampire because it's frozen into sharp points like fangs. We'll head there and maybe I'll remember more on the way.'

I feel a rush of optimism. Mitch sounds so calm and confident that us beating Crowky to The Box seems like a possibility again. I want to get going straight away. 'Whose ship shall we take?' I say.

Mitch laughs. 'Well, mine *obviously*, because yours is rubbish.'

We look over at the *Bowt* bobbing up and down in the water, its pants flag flapping in the wind. 'I suppose yours is bigger,' admits Rose.

'And it hasn't got a face,' says Mitch. 'But I'm afraid we're going to have to do a bit of pillaging before we set sail. It's nothing personal, just how us pirates do things: we nick stuff then share it out.' With a loud bellow she gives an order that makes her crew of orangutans drop what they're doing and go leaping across the net to the *Bowt*.

'Can I go and get some pick 'n' mix?' asks Win, a note of panic in his voice.

Mitch shrugs. 'Sure, but you'll have to fight them for it.'

'Wish me luck!' he cries, then with a whoop he pulls out his wooden sword and goes clambering across the net.

Mitch grins. 'This should be fun,' she says, then she settles back in her hot tub, ready to watch a ninja wizard fight a load of apes for sweets.

'Get me some rocky road!' I shout as Win dodges an orangutan's fist and disappears below deck.

***

Once all the pillaging is over, and Win has returned bruised but triumphant, his pockets bulging with sweets, we say goodbye to the honey badgers. Mitch invited them to join her crew but Danny and Eric were keen to head off alone and sail north beyond The End to try their luck on the Slushy Seas, whatever they are.

'I'm still your captain!' Rose calls after them as our two ships slip apart. At least, that's what she claims she said. To me it sounded like a load of growls.

It's sad to say goodbye to our strange ship, and our even stranger crew, but as the *Alisha*'s sails fill with wind it's obvious we've made the right decision. The *Alisha* is fast, and soon we're racing across the sea. Plus it feels good knowing we're on board a ship that's bigger than the *Raven* and captained by a witch.

Mitch announces that we are going to sail through the night to make up for lost time. I offer to help on the rigging, but it's clear the orangutans don't want me getting under their feet. So, while the sun sets, I lean back against Mitch's hot tub (I have to, it's freezing) and start to map The End.

Using paper and a pen borrowed from Mitch, I draw the line of mountains we sailed through and everything I can see ahead of us. I carefully draw the strange creatures I've already spotted: a huge, fluffy white whale, a whole gang of flying penguins, and some sort of manatee that I thought was a blob of seaweed until it lifted its head out of the water and started mewing.

There's a bang as Mitch opens the trapdoor from her cabin. She drops into her hot tub, has a quick swim under the water then comes to see what I'm doing. 'That

165

mountain's way bigger,' she says, leaving a wet fingerprint on my map. 'And tomorrow you'll see that the islands are pointier . . . but I suppose this is all new to you.'

It is all new to me, but at the same time it feels strangely familiar, and I think I know why. Now we're sailing through this world of pirate ships and whales and snow, I'm starting to wonder if it was mainly *my* ideas that got sent to The End. After all, it was me who was into pirates, and me who was obsessed with all things snowy. I've watched *Frozen Planet* loads of times and one Christmas I got the book and a cuddly baby seal. I used to pretend that seal was a killer whale and make it destroy boats full of Lego people.

Just then one of the furry whales arcs out of the water, racing alongside the ship. It fixes us with a small eye, shoots a fountain of glittering water from its blowhole then disappears beneath the waves again.

'The orangutans reckon they can swallow you whole,' says Mitch with delight. Then she sighs, 'I love it here!'

'Me too,' I say, and I realise this is true. My fingers might be aching and the air is so cold it's hurting my lungs, but I feel happy in this world of ice and snow. I guess that's because I made most of it.

'Wait until you see the Vampire,' says Mitch, and she bares her teeth at me and hisses.

'Are you being a vampire?'

'Yes,' she says, laughing, then she throws herself back in her hot tub and stares up at the stars.

CHAPTER 32

While Rose sleeps in Mitch's cabin, Win and I share a dark, low-ceilinged room with the orangutans. They snuffle and snore, but at least their furry bodies keep the room warm.

It's Win who wakes me up. 'Arthur!' he cries, shaking my hammock. 'You've *got* to see where we are. It's so cool and SO COLD!'

I pull on my onesie and stumble after him on to the deck.

The bitter icy cold hits me first, stealing my breath away, then I'm dazzled by bright light. I shove my hands deep into the pockets of my onesie and join Rose at the railing.

We're moored in a curving bay surrounded by towering mountains. The sea around us is slushy with ice and larger sheets knock against the side of the ship.

'Amazing, isn't it?' she says.

I nod. It's all I can do. I'm too cold to speak. Instead I let my eyes run over the rocky shoreline. Beyond it lies a forest

of snow-covered trees that has a path running through it. No, not a path; a river – a band of blue sparkling ice which leads from the sea to a gigantic waterfall.

And this is what Rose is staring at.

The waterfall is frozen. Great blue icicles point towards the ground as if the water was gushing one moment then froze the next. Two of the icicles are bigger than the others and they form sharp, curving points.

'The Vampire,' I say, my breath making a cloud in the air. Just then something soft lands on my nose. I look up and see that the sky is bulging with clouds. A few more snowflakes settle on my face. Except for the sound of our breath and the creaking ice, thick silence surrounds us.

'You've not seen it, have you?' Rose's voice is a whisper.

'Seen what?'

She points at a narrow gap between two cliffs. Crowky's tall ship, the *Raven*, is tucked inside it, almost invisible. It dips up and down with the waves. The sails are hauled in and the deck is deserted.

The sight of it makes my skin prickle with fear. I pull my onesie closer to me and look around. I scan the forest and the base of the mountains. I blink into the light, looking for any sign of Crowky.

'I've not seen him or any scarecrows,' says Rose.

'But he's here,' I say. My eyes flick back to the forest, looking for moving shapes, footprints, any sign of life. Could he have already found The Box? Is he dragging it out of some cave or hole right now?

'We need to work out where Mitch hid The Box, and we need to do it now,' I say. 'Then we get out of here.'

Rose nods, but then she says, 'He's always one step ahead of us, Arthur.'

This is new. It's usually me who says things like this, not Rose. 'But we've got Mitch,' I say, 'the person who actually hid The Box. He's just got the tattoo. Come on. Let's see if she's remembered anything.'

We find Mitch and Win in the captain's cabin. Rose must have given her back her tattoo kit because Mitch is floating in her bath, brushing a feather over the tip of her little finger. Pink smoke rises in the air.

'What do you think?' she says, wiggling her finger. 'It's a rosebud because I found you, Rose.'

'I love it,' says Rose, but she only manages a small smile.

Win is over by the shelves, looking through Mitch's ingredients. He picks up a jar of murky water and goes to open it, but before he can unscrew the lid Mitch has tapped some grains on to the palm of her hand and blown them in his direction. Frost rushes over his fingers, freezing them to the jar.

'Oww!' he complains. 'Will you stop doing that?'

'Only if you stop touching my stuff.'

'We've got a job to do,' says Rose, reaching past the bath and opening the window of the cabin. A flurry of snow drifts in. From here we have a perfect view of the frozen waterfall with its two sharp teeth. 'The Box is out there, somewhere, and we've got to find it.'

'Yeah, but I don't know what this means, do I?' says Mitch, propping herself up next to Rose and pushing up a wet sleeve. We stare at the tattoo.

'Together we can work it out,' says Rose. 'We have to get to The Box before Crowky. Arthur and I are older now and our worries are different.'

Mitch narrows her eyes. 'Different how?'

'They're bad, Mitch, trust me,' says Rose. 'They're the kind of things we can't say out loud.'

Mitch nods. 'Let's do it then.'

The four of us gaze at the picture. 'We're in the right place because that's obviously the Vampire,' says Rose, pointing at the two curving teeth. Our eyes move from the picture to the real thing. 'And the mountains are the same, and so is the river . . . but it's hard to see where The Box is supposed to be.'

'That thing looks like an arrow.' Win points at the symbol pointing towards The Box. 'Or is it a tree?'

I look out of the window. 'But that doesn't make any sense. It means The Box is hidden at the bottom of the sea.'

'Maybe it is!' says Mitch. 'I mean, I am a *mer*witch.'

We agree that Mitch should go and search the seabed. She does this happily, diving straight out of the window and into the sea. We go on deck and for the next few hours we keep a look out for Crowky and his scarecrows, but also for Mitch. At any moment she could swim to the surface with The Box. That would be brilliant, but it would be dangerous too, because we're sure that Crowky is watching us. It *feels* like he's watching us.

Occasionally Mitch's head pops out of the water, but she's just coming up for air. Eventually she climbs back on board using a long knotted rope, then throws herself into the hot tub.

'So?' I say. 'Did you see it?'

Light snow is falling. Flakes land on the water and melt away. Mitch rubs her arms. I notice her teeth are chattering. 'There's nothing down there,' she says, 'and I mean nothing at all. It's just smooth sand. I've searched the whole bay.'

'Maybe you buried it,' says Win.

She shakes her head. 'I thought of that, but how would it stay down there? There's nothing I could tie it to, or wedge it in. It must be somewhere else.'

'And we'll find it,' says Rose. 'We just need to look again.'

So that's what we do. We go back to Mitch's cabin and look from Mitch's tattoo to the window. Win wants us to go to shore and 'have a dig around', but the cove is big. There's no way we could search the miles of forest that lie in front of us, and we know that if we leave the ship, Crowky could get us. Here we're protected.

As the day wears on, our ideas become wilder and

wilder. Win even suggests that The Box could be hidden at the top of the mountain, and that Mitch got a group of penguins to fly it up there for her. This makes Mitch throw a book at him and yell, 'WORST SUGGESTION EVER, WININJA!'

It isn't just Mitch who's starting to lose her temper. As minutes and then hours tick by, Rose and I get jumpier too. We know that Crowky is probably doing exactly what we're doing – staring at the tattoo and trying to work out where The Box is hidden – and possibly he's doing it more successfully than we are. This isn't a good thought.

'The problem is,' I say, 'Crowky is clever.'

'You don't need to keep telling us, Arthur,' snaps Rose.

But as night falls, and we're still no closer to finding The Box, I start to wonder what would jump out if my name appeared on the side. Would it be some sort of guide that leads Crowky to the tunnel? Or a creature that can fly him to the waterfall? Or maybe letters will appear in the sky spelling out: GRANDAD'S T-SHIRT WILL LET YOU IN!

My mind is stuck on a horrible loop of Crowky finding his way to Home, then creeping down Grandad's stairs, his stick fingers twitchy with excitement. Where would Grandad be? Sitting at his kitchen table eating cereal? Pottering around his garden? And then Crowky appears . . .

I shake my head. I've got to stop this.

Mitch finishes her potion, pours it into a dish and sets fire to it. Blue flames dance over the top. It looks like a

Christmas pudding. 'What are you making?' I ask. 'Some sort of memory potion?'

'No,' she says. 'Just some pretty flames.'

'Cool!' says Win, then he magics up some blue stars and soon the magic competition begins again, only this time, it's blue-themed.

As blue snow floats over us, I join Rose at the window. She's staring at the waterfall. Her freckles stand out against her brown skin and her hands are curled into fists.

'We can find it, can't we, Rose?' I say.

She turns to look at me. 'We have no choice. We have to.'

CHAPTER 33

When a sea mist hides the shore from view, and the last of the light fades from the sky, we decide to give up for the night. To be honest, Mitch and Win gave up a while ago.

Aware of just how close Crowky could be, we agree to take it in turns to be on watch.

Win and I volunteer to go first and I find myself standing at the prow of the ship, surrounded by mist and armed with a bell. Win went off ten minutes ago to get us a hot drink and I haven't seen him since.

I can't see anything, so instead I listen carefully for the sound of oars cutting through water. We're sure Crowky can't fly – when we spotted him on the *Raven* he had to glide and use ropes to get down from the crow's nest – so if he does try to get on board he'll have to approach by boat. I try to listen, but the *Alisha* is groaning and clinking and the mist makes it hard to concentrate.

I pull my hood low and watch as the mist slips between

the railings of the gunwale and creeps across the deck. I've got a lamp that I've hung from a hook and I'm standing in its circle of dim light. This should be comforting, but instead I feel like a spotlight is shining down on me.

To distract myself, I picture the tattoo, and I try to see what we've missed. A sharp creak makes me spin round, but I'm staring into a wall of mist. 'Win? Is that you?'

Silence.

I remind myself that the *Alisha* is always creaking. Mitch says the ship's made of old bones, although I'm fairly certain she's just trying to freak me out.

I hear another creak followed by another. Footsteps . . . Fear slips through me as quickly as the mist that's twisting round my ankles.

'Win!' I shout, reaching out with my hands. 'Where are you?'

I'm not sure which way I'm facing now, towards the ship or the sea. This is stupid. How can I be on watch if I can't see? I start to move forward, my arms outstretched, feeling for a railing or mast, anything that will help me work out where I am.

A dark shape appears in the corner of my eye. Shock makes me gasp and drop the bell. Then, before I can scream or run or do anything, stick fingers wrap round my face, digging into my skin and covering my eyes.

'Hello, Arthur Trout!' Crowky's voice is a rusty snarl. 'Don't bother trying to escape because I've *got you!*'

I try to shout and wriggle out of his grasp, but he's right. His fingers have already begun to do their work.

'*Drain*,' he whispers in my ear. '*Drain . . .*'

Cold locks my legs to the deck of the ship and begins to climb through my body. Any warmth I had left is slipping out of me and being replaced with a cold, prickly emptiness. Crowky is stuffing me, turning me into a scarecrow, and there's nothing I can do about it. Again, I try to struggle, but I can barely move my lips. I just manage to whisper, '*Win.*'

'No one is coming.' His voice is close to my ear.

I want to curl my fingers but they're spreading out and fixing in place like sticks.

Crowky takes his hands away from my face then lifts my arms like he's a puppeteer. My body is locked solid to the deck of the ship, my arms outstretched. He steps in front of me. 'Perfect,' he says.

I try to shrink away, but I can't. Crowky's face is round and made of sack. His eyes are moving, shifting buttons. His mouth is stitched and loose threads float in the freezing night air. With every movement he makes I hear the rustle of straw, and this straw bursts from the top of his head as pale wild hair.

His smile gets bigger. A pair of black wings begins to unfold from his shoulders until feathers brush the deck. They're still damaged, burnt and tattered in places, but new feathers have begun to grow back. He pushes back his shoulders and his coat gapes open. To my horror I realise that he's wearing Grandad's T-shirt. Small stitches criss-cross rips in the fabric, holding it together.

Crowky reaches forward, grabs the front of my onesie and pulls me closer. 'What's in the box, Arthur?' He laughs and the coldness that's been creeping through my body reaches my face.

'Not . . . scared . . .' I whisper.

It's a lie and Crowky knows it. His laugh gets louder, his grip tighter. 'Have you ever wanted something just because you're not allowed it, Arthur Trout?' I don't reply. I can't.

'I have,' he says, ramming his face into mine, 'and you know what it is, don't you? *Home.*'

He pauses to let his words sink in, his eyes locked on to mine.

'After you stole the Crow's Nest from me, I had time to think, and I realised there must be something very precious in Home for you to guard it so carefully. What is it, Arthur?' He stares deep into my eyes. Snow falls on us. It lands on his feathers and my face. 'Is it your *grandad?*' He taps a twig finger on my chest where my heart is. 'Are there other precious things there too? Starting with your grandad, I'm going to find those things you love and take them away from you, just like you took *my* home away from *me.*'

Keeping one hand gripped round my chin he reaches into his leather coat and pulls out a piece of paper. I recognise it immediately. 'You know how I'm going to get to Home, don't you?'

I stare at the image I know so well: the fang-like teeth of the frozen waterfall, the drop of water, the small box with the fish drawn inside it. Crowky thrusts it into my face. 'The Box will show me the way. I just have to wait for your name to appear and then it will happen, because *my* dream is *your* nightmare! We just need to find it. We're close, aren't we? I wonder who will get there first?'

Then he squeezes my face, turning it round. I refuse to look at him. It's the only thing I can do to fight back. Instead I stare into the distance. The mist is beginning to clear. It drifts away from the moon. Moonlight falls on the glittering waterfall, the frozen river and the forest. One tree at the edge of the forest is bigger than the others. It rises above them like an arrow pointing to the sky. The moonlight shines on this too.

Crowky yanks my face back, forcing our eyes to meet. '*What's in the box, Arthur?*' he hisses.

'Arthur?' Win's voice drifts through the mist. In a flash Crowky lets go of me, beats his wings and shoots up in the air. He grabs a rope, swings over the side of the ship, and then he's gone.

The next thing I know Win is throwing his arms round my middle and squeezing me tight. 'It was Crowky, wasn't it?' he says, as my head and then my arms flop down. Win's hands push away the coldness and I feel my heart beat faster. My knees buckle under me and Win catches me before I fall. 'Rose!' he shouts. 'ROSE!'

I hear more footsteps, then Rose is pressing her hands down on me too. 'He was here,' says Win. 'Crowky was here. I saw him!'

'Arthur?' Rose shakes me hard. 'Arthur? Are you OK?'

I flop back on the deck and lift a shaking arm. I point at the shore, at the tall tree that's still lit up by the moon. 'Found it,' I whisper before darkness falls over me.

CHAPTER 34

I come round in Mitch's cabin. Rose and Win must have dragged me here and now they're trying to warm me up with blankets, extra logs on the fire and their own hands.

'Come on, Arthur!' Rose is clutching my wrist while Win rubs my fingers between his hands. Mitch is by her cauldron, sprinkling something black into a bubbling mixture.

'He's awake!' says Win.

Rose squeezes my wrist even tighter. 'What did Crowky want, Arthur? And what did you mean when you said *found it?*'

I try to talk, but no words come out. My throat feels as dry as straw.

'He's still half stuffed,' says Mitch, pressing a glass of hot fizzing liquid into my hands. 'Give him a minute.'

They watch as I sip at the drink. Slowly heat returns to my body: the tips of my toes, my ears, my nose. The middle of my chest still feels like a cold rock, but the pain has begun to melt away.

'If feels rough, doesn't it?' says Mitch. 'It happened to me once when Crowky kidnapped me. It felt like I'd been emptied out and filled with prickly ice.'

I take another sip of the drink, then I manage to say, 'I know where it is.'

'You know where *what* is?' says Rose.

'The Box!'

'Really?' Rose exchanges a look with Mitch and Win. Clearly they think my mind's still stuffed and that I'm not thinking straight.

'Yes!' I struggle to sit up. 'I'll show you. Win, open the windows.'

He throws them open, letting in the icy air. The mist has almost gone and the moon lights up the whole bay; the snow-topped trees, the mountains and the sea are all bathed in yellow light.

'Show us the map, Mitch.'

She pulls up her sleeve and I point at the arrow leading to The Box. 'This isn't an arrow,' I say. 'It's a *shadow*. Look out of the window and you'll see.'

Moonlight shines down on the trees, casting shadows on to the white snow. The tall tree at the edge of the forest has a shadow that stretches across the snow and the sea, pointing towards a small island. It looks exactly like an arrow.

The tattoo, the moonlit scene outside the window . . . they're identical. Crowky wanted to scare me and make sure the right fear was planted in my mind, and it worked. But he also showed me where The Box was hidden.

'The Box must be on that island!' cries Rose.

I grab Win's telescope and go to the window. 'It's not an island,' I say. 'Not now anyway. The sea around it is frozen, joining it to the land.'

'But if I'd come when the sea was warmer I could have got there,' says Mitch, and for a moment we stare at the moonlit island where we are sure The Box is hidden.

'We should go now,' I say, remembering Crowky's frantic energy, certain that since he left me he hasn't stopped thinking about The Box. 'If we're quick, we can get The Box and be back before dawn. The *Alisha* is faster than the *Raven*. We can easily outrun Crowky!' I'm imagining getting back to Win's cave and spending the rest of the holiday as I'd planned – lazy days riding dragons, swimming and exploring every corner of Roar.

'This is our chance to get ahead of Crowky,' says Rose. 'Once we've got The Box we can take you home, Mitch!'

'Home,' she says, smiling. 'I would love that.'

Suddenly everything seems within our reach, and I'm so sure that we're going to get to The Box before Crowky that right now I don't even care what's inside it. Win, filled with the excitement of the moment, pulls out his wand and shouts, 'Whistle fur!' and a clutch of marshmallows burst from the end of his wand, falling over us like snow.

'There is one problem,' says Rose. 'The moon's so bright that Crowky will see us rowing to shore.'

'Leave that to me,' says Mitch, picking a marshmallow out of her hair and popping it in her mouth. 'I'll conjure up something awesome to hide the boat.' Then she selects a bottle from the shelf and shakes it. 'Maybe I'll bring the mist back, or make a snow storm.' She pulls the cork out with her teeth and starts shaking white drops into her cauldron.

I try to be patient as Mitch mixes and stirs. I tighten my laces and pull up the hood on my onesie. Win does a few ninja moves, annoying Mitch by bumping into her and making her drop a handful of fish into her potion.

Rose just stares out of the window, her eyes fixed on the shadow that points to the island.

CHAPTER 35

Mitch swims ahead of us, pulling the rowing boat through a blizzard of fat snowflakes. Her spell has worked brilliantly and snow is falling heavily.

She turns to look at us. 'I can't see a thing,' she whispers, scowling at Win. 'Far too many herring went in the cauldron.' Then she slips back into the water and the boat starts moving again.

'I *helped*,' protests Win. 'There's no way Crowky will be able to see us in this.'

He's right. The snow may be heavy and cold, but it totally hides us from view. I just hope Mitch's spell lasts until we've found The Box and got back to the *Alisha*. Plus, dawn is coming. Through the swirling snow I can see that the sky is starting to lighten.

The boat bumps against ice. There were too many rocks around the island for us to land there, so Mitch has brought us as close as we can get. We'll walk through the forest and get to the island that way. Hopefully

Mitch will join us there.

Her head bobs back up. 'Remember: when you get to the trees walk *west*.'

'Be careful,' says Rose.

Mitch laughs at the idea that something could happen to her. Frost is dusted across her eyelashes and hair. Her lips are blue from the cold. 'It's you three who need to be careful,' she says. 'This is The End. I've not been sailing these waters long, but I can tell you it's a strange place. And remember: Crowky is *close*.'

How could we forget? We climb out, then Mitch disappears under the water and starts pulling the boat back out to sea.

'This way,' says Rose, and she leads us across the slippery ice that hugs the shore. Once we get to land, Rose reaches into Mitch's bag and pulls out a compass. We trudge forward. *So this is The End*, I think as my feet sink into the deep snow. I should want to explore, but right now all I want to do is get The Box and get out of here.

We reach the forest and walk between tall trees. Their branches are heavy with snow and occasionally a clump falls to the ground, making us jump. But except for this, and our crunching footsteps, the forest is eerily silent.

The trees start to thin and Rose comes to a sudden stop. 'We're here,' she whispers.

We've reached the sea and in front of us lies the island. It's like a scene from a snow globe: whirling snow falls on a domed island dotted with fir trees. Thick ice stretches from where we're standing to craggy rocks. Behind us is the tall tree I saw from the deck of the *Alisha*; its shadow makes a path that leads directly to the island.

'Let's go,' I say as the three of us step on to the ice. 'Let's find The Box and get rid of it once and for all.'

We take tentative steps forward. 'But *how* will we get rid of it?' asks Win. 'I mean, we never managed it before.'

Sometimes I wish Win would keep his thoughts inside his head. 'Well, we will this time,' I say. 'We can take it back to Home or get Bad Dragon to eat it. We'll think of something.'

Win puts his arm round my shoulders. 'I know you will,' he says with total confidence.

We reach the island and split up. Soon our footsteps have made intricate patterns in the snow as we run backward and forward searching for The Box. We look under the trees, kick snow away from the base of rocks and Win even climbs to the top of the tallest tree to check in the branches.

I'm just starting to wonder if I could have been wrong about this island when I hear a hear a loud *crack* coming from the frozen sea. A moment later a rock and some golden sparks shoot through the ice and Mitch's face pops out of the hole. She takes enormous gasping breaths as she pulls herself on to the ice. 'Blimey,' she says, laughing and sucking on her webbed fingers, 'that was cold. So where's

The Box? I thought you'd have it by now.'

'We can't find it,' says Rose, trying to hide the panic in her voice.

'Any idea where you might have put it?' shouts Win from up in the tree.

'SHHHH!' we say.

'SORRY!' he yells back.

Mitch pulls herself next to us and studies the island. She shakes her head. 'I'm sorry. I haven't got a clue.'

I'm just wondering when we should give up – we don't want the snow to clear and reveal our hiding place to Crowky – when Win shouts, 'I'VE GOT IT!'

'SHHHH!' we say again, but he ignores us, slithers out of the tree and runs to a pile of rocks.

'Mitch, show us your tattoo,' says Win.

Once again Mitch pushes up her shirt sleeve, only it's difficult this time because the fabric has frozen into stiff folds.

Win points at the cross that marks the fish's eye. '*This* is where it's hidden!' he says. 'Up in the tree I could see that this island is shaped like a fish, and those rocks over there –' he waves at a clump of rocks sitting in the water – 'they make a fishy tail, and these –' he pauses here to pat the rocks – 'are where its eye should be.'

'Huh,' says Mitch, staring at her own tattoo. Then she looks up and grins. 'X marks the spot! I'm a genius!'

We don't waste another moment. We start scooping up

189

handfuls of snow and digging around the base of the rocks. Then Rose hisses, 'I can feel something!'

Together, we push snow out of the way until smooth surfaces are revealed. I wipe off the last layer of snow, and suddenly there it is: a very ordinary cardboard box wedged into a hole in the rock.

Win laughs and throws a handful of snow up in the air, but Rose and I just sit and stare. The Box is a beautiful, terrifying sight. The jolly goldfish smiles at us. Carefully we dig around the edges until Mitch is able to slide it out. 'It's so light,' she says. 'Are you sure there's something in there?'

'If there's not something in there now, there will be soon,' I say. I've been keeping a close watch on The Box, looking for any sign of glimmering letters. Rose and I only had to be near The Box for the words to appear, but right now it's

just a plain, brown cardboard box.

'I wish the lid wasn't so loose,' I say. It looks dangerously flappy and we've got no Sellotape or string to hold it down. Win and Mitch wouldn't open it, but what if the words appear and we drop it, or it falls open by accident?

'Don't worry about that,' says Rose. 'Let's get out of here. The snow is slowing down.'

I look up. Now there's only a light dusting of snow falling and we've still got to walk through the forest and get back to the *Alisha*.

'Mitch, can you make any more?' I say.

She rifles through the amulets she's strung round her neck, pulls out a bronze bottle and shakes the contents on to a handful of snow. A few red drops fall like blood. 'That's all I've got left,' she says, then she blows it from her fingers straight into the sky. It whirls around and around, and more snow starts to fall, but it's nothing like the storm she produced earlier.

Mitch wriggles back towards her hole in the ice. 'You'd better be quick,' she says as she slips into the water. 'I'll get the boat and meet you at the shore!'

CHAPTER 36

We leave the island and walk back across the frozen sea. Rose carries The Box in front of her as carefully as if it were a baby. We speed up when we get to the forest, desperate to reach the safety of the ship, following our footprints from earlier. Our breath mists the air. *Like dragons*, I think, wishing one of the dragons was with us now, protecting us and filling this frozen world with fire.

Rose comes to a sudden stop.

'What is it?' I say. We're almost back at the shore. I can see the boat bobbing around. Mitch must be there, waiting for us.

Rose looks from left to right. 'I thought I heard something.'

'Me too,' says Win. 'It was just snow falling, wasn't it?'

Rose shakes her head. 'No, it sounded more like . . . *feathers*.'

'Stop it, Rose.' I say. 'This place is creepy enough as it is. You're imagining things.'

She nods, letting me pull her forward, her hands still wrapped round The Box.

But then something catches my eye. Sitting hunched in the branches of a tree is a figure. My heart seems to stop beating as a pale face grins down at me. 'RUN!' I shout, but already Crowky is leaping from the tree. He glides to the ground, wings spread wide, and lands, blocking our path.

We spin round, ready to race back the way we've come, but we've only taken a few steps when we realise that something is happening to the trees. They're trembling and moving.

'What's going on?' I say as clumps of snow tumble to the ground. Then outstretched arms and stick fingers appear and heavy sack heads swing from side to side, scattering snow in all directions.

'It's the scarecrow army!' yells Rose.

They've been waiting for us, hidden among the trees and disguised by the snow.

Crowky makes a clicking noise and the scarecrows start to step closer until they've formed a circle around us. Then they stand there, staring, their tattered clothes floating in the wind.

Crowky's eyes are fixed on The Box.

'You've been here the whole time, haven't you?' I say.

He nods and laughs. 'Thank you for the snowstorm. It hid us beautifully.'

I shiver to think that we walked right through the pack

of scarecrows, and the whole time Crowky was up in that tree watching us. But something doesn't make sense. The bay is huge and so is the forest. How did Crowky know where to hide his army? Then I remember what happened on the deck of the *Alisha*: Crowky holding the map and then grabbing my face and turning it. He was showing me where to look!

'You *knew* where The Box was hidden,' I say.

'Not quite,' he admits. 'I knew it was somewhere on the island, but I decided to let the Masters of Roar find it and bring it to me. After all, I need you for the next bit, don't I?'

He whistles then clicks. Several scarecrows break away

from the others and move towards us. 'No!' shouts Rose, and we squeeze even closer together as her arms wrap round The Box.

Win pulls out his wand. 'Egg-tremble!' he shouts. 'EGG-TREMBLE!' A flame leaps from his wand. It's good, it really is, but the scarecrows simply jump to one side, avoiding it, then one of them snatches the wand from Win, snaps it and tosses it to the ground.

Then they turn on us. A scarecrow in a tattered dress grabs Win by his cloak and another towers over me. Her twig fingers wrap round my shoulders and I'm wrenched away from The Box. Rose manages to fight them off for longer. She clings on to The Box, until two scarecrows pounce on her, grabbing hold of her hair and face. With a scream, she lets The Box fall into the snow.

A bellow of rage echoes from the shore. Mitch is pulling herself on to the ice. Her hands reach for a bottle round her neck. She crushes the glass in her bare hands and throws the whole lot up in the air, smacking it with her tail. A blast of wind races towards us, blowing snow from the trees and hitting us hard. But the scarecrows are too strong. They hold their ground, tightening their grip, while Crowky sends more of them after her.

'Get out of here!' Rose shouts to her friend. 'Get back to the ship. Make a spell!'

Mitch hesitates. Her eyes dart from us to the scarecrows who are racing closer. At the last moment, she comes to a decision and dives back into the water, disappearing from sight.

Crowky turns and gazes at The Box with greedy eyes.

'Don't touch it!' says Rose, but he ignores her and runs his twig fingers across the lid.

His wings tremble. Rose lurches forward and he looks up. 'It's mine now, Rose.' Then he laughs as if he can't quite believe this is true.

He signals to the scarecrows holding us. They toss us down in the snow then step back to join the others. As one, the scarecrows raise their arms and fall still. Snow dusts their drooping heads. They've formed a cage, and we're trapped inside.

Suddenly Crowky gasps with delight. A glimmer of light has appeared on the side of The Box.

CHAPTER 37

Everything seems to freeze: my breath, Crowky's fingers, even the air around us. The ice groans and my chest squeezes tight with cold and fear. Rose, Win and I huddle together as the golden letters form words.

What's in the box . . .

The writing pauses. I feel weak at the knees, sick. Rose's fingers find mine and for the first time in years we hold hands. The writing begins again with a large sweeping 'R'.

I feel a rush of giddy relief. It's not me. Crowky won't get to Home, not yet anyway! He must realise this too because a flash of anger crosses his face.

Then a question mark gleams and the message is complete.

What's in the box, Rose?

Rose's fingers slip out of mine and my relief is replaced by guilt. Crowky cackles. 'What's in the box, *Rose*? Tell us!'

'I don't know.' Her voice is tight with panic.

'Then let's find out.'

'NO!' I shout, but already he's opening the lid.

We stare at The Box as snow falls gently around us. Nothing happens. The golden words fade away, and I have this brilliant moment when I think, *it's stopped working! Nothing's coming out!*

Then we hear a soft, low growl. It echoes around the clearing. It slips between the trees. It floats on the air and creeps inside me, making the hairs on my neck prickle. The growl is coming from The Box.

A snout and then two grey ears appear. The top of a head follows, huge and thick with fur. It's some sort of animal. Two yellow eyes peer out. They slide from left to right, then settle on Rose.

'It's a *wolf*,' I say. But this doesn't make any sense. Rose isn't scared of wolves; in fact, they're one of her favourite animals. She's even got this sweatshirt she bought from a shop on the pier with a wolf's face on it!

The wolf sniffs the air – eyes still on Rose – and a sly smile creeps across its face.

Rose laughs nervously. 'That's not my fear. Look at it. It's beautiful!'

The wolf leaps effortlessly from The Box and drops down in the snow. It pauses, then pads towards Rose. It stops in front of her, its head hanging from gigantic shoulders. 'Hello,' she says, reaching out a hand.

The wolf wrinkles its nose, curls its lips over sharp teeth and snarls. Saliva flies into the air and Rose shrinks back. Crowky is watching this with a look of delight. His hands are clenched and his wings are open and beating the air.

'Ignore it, Rose.' I grab her arm. 'Look at me. Pretend it isn't here!'

'It's hard, Arthur. It's big!'

The wolf stretches its head back and howls into the sky. Rose huddles between me and Win. 'It's just one wolf, Rose,' I say. 'You've tamed dragons. I bet you could tame a wolf too!'

Then Win says, 'Something else is coming out.'

It's another wolf, only this one is almost white, and its eyes are pale grey. It jumps from The Box and trots straight towards Rose. As the growling begins again, another shaggy head appears. How many are there? This one is the biggest so far and it's scrabbling at the cardboard. It leaps through the air and dashes towards Rose. Then two more jump out, followed by another. Now there are six wolves – a pack.

They start to circle us, mouths gaping, saliva dripping on to the snow. 'I don't think these wolves want to be tamed,' says Rose, her voice shaky.

She's right. They look like they want to attack.

'Look,' says Rose, 'there's something else.'

Another pair of ears has poked out of The Box, but they don't belong to a wolf; at least, not any more. They're part of a hat. A face appears, then hands encased in leather gloves grab the side of The Box.

'It's a girl!' says Win as she clambers out and jumps into the snow. If he thinks this will reassure Rose, he's wrong. The sight of her makes Rose shrink even closer to us.

She dusts snow off her coat and stares at Rose from under her fur hat. Her eyes are pale blue, like ice, and her hair is thick, dirty and matted. She's wearing fur-lined boots and has a belt buckled tight round her coat. She raises her sunburnt face and I see scratches running down her neck.

'Rose, who is she?' I say.

'I don't know!'

The girl whistles and instantly the circling wolves fall still. 'I'm Hati Skoll,' she says. Her voice is loud and hard; it rises over the wolves' growls. 'Where am I?'

'You're in the Land of Roar,' says Win. 'It belongs to Rose and Arthur Trout, and your wolves are getting right in their faces!'

Hati shrugs. 'I don't care who it belongs to. I'm here to hunt.'

Her last words hang in the air. Snow falls quietly around us.

'And *what* are you hunting?' says Crowky.

Hati looks at us, then she lifts a finger and points it at Rose. 'Her.'

The wolves creep towards Rose, snapping their teeth. Hati moves closer too. 'Rose Trout, you have a choice,' she says. 'You can come with me and join my pack, or you can try to escape. If you choose to run, we will hunt you down, but if you join us, you will have nothing to fear.'

'Oh yes she will,' Crowky says. 'She will have *me* to fear, and so will you!' Wings stretched wide, he lurches towards Hati.

She whistles and three wolves slam Crowky down in the snow where he struggles briefly, feathers flying in the air. Then he falls still. On the edge of the clearing the scarecrow army curl their hands into fists. They're waiting for Crowky's signal to attack, but something stops him. His eyes dart to The Box. That's all he cares about. He wants my fear more than anything.

The side of The Box is still smooth and blank. There

are no gleaming letters, but as long as The Box is close to me and Rose there's a chance they will appear.

Hati calls her wolves off. Crowky shuffles backwards, grabbing hold of The Box and holding it close.

The wolves start circling us again. 'Well?' says Hati. 'What are you going to do, Rose Trout? Join us, or be hunted down?'

I grab Rose's arm. 'Don't listen to her, Rose. She's your fear, remember? We have to run.'

'And you won't be on your own,' adds Win. 'You'll have me and Arthur with you!'

This almost makes Rose smile. 'Win, how can you protect me from a pack of wolves?'

'I'll use my ninja skills,' he says.

Now Rose does smile. It's a small smile, but it feels like a victory against Hati Skoll. And maybe she senses this too because she stamps her foot and says, 'What's your decision?'

Rose's voice is a whisper. 'I'm going to run.'

Hati is incredulous. 'You really think these *boys* can help you?'

'Yes,' says Rose.

'Then you'd better start running. I'll give you one minute each. That's three minutes to get as far away as possible.'

'What . . . You're letting us go?' I say.

Hati shrugs. 'Unless it's a fair chase, it's no fun.'

The wolves strain towards us, whining and snapping. 'Not yet . . .' she says, her hands keeping them back. 'Not yet . . .'

Suddenly a bright light catches my eye. It's The Box. The writing is starting to appear. We have to get out of here before the message is complete. 'RUN!' I shout, and the three of us dodge past the wolves and the waiting scarecrows. Win spies his half-snapped wand sticking out of the snow and grabs it.

We head towards the waterfall. We have no choice. If we run towards the sea we'll be trapped. Out of the corner of my eye I see Crowky creeping away with The Box.

'Whistle fur!' Win cries, waving his wand over his shoulder and sending a shower of marshmallows towards Hati and the wolves.

'Why did you do that?' I shout.

'Cool parting gesture!' he yells.

Rose groans, and slipping and sliding in the thick snow we run as fast as we can towards the gaping teeth of the Vampire.

CHAPTER 38

We clamber over the slippery rocks at the base of the waterfall. Somewhere behind us the wolves howl, but they're not chasing us yet.

The frozen teeth look bigger close up, the size of tree trunks. To get inside we're going to have to squeeze between them. We find the biggest gap and Rose goes first, then Win follows. Suddenly a whistle pierces the air, and the wolves stop howling. Then the barking begins.

I glance back. The wolves are racing across the snow, heading towards us. 'Hurry up!' I shout. 'They're coming!' I push my way between the icicles and stumble after Win.

'This way,' says Rose, and she starts running towards the back of the cave which becomes a tunnel. Win and I follow.

'I seriously hope this tunnel goes somewhere!' says Win as the barking becomes louder.

Rose comes to an abrupt stop and we almost run into the back of her. The tunnel splits in three directions. The passages leading left and right look wide and flat, but the opening directly in front of us plunges down steeply. It's more a chute than a tunnel.

Behind us we hear skittering paws. The growls and barks get louder.

'Which way shall we go?' I say.

'It doesn't matter,' says Rose. 'We can't outrun them. It's impossible!'

A howl fills the cave. The first wolf has pushed his head inside the cave.

'This way,' says Win, and he aims for the middle tunnel. Immediately his feet slip out from under him and he crashes to the ground. He spins round once, twice, then disappears down the chute with a wild scream.

I look back. The mouth of the Vampire is blocked by fighting furry bodies. The wolves snap and snarl, desperate to get past the teeth and each other, and get to Rose. Win's scream trails off. I don't have time to think about whether he's been whisked to safety or fallen down an icy crevasse because a wolf has got through and is running straight towards us. The rest follow, a mass of thick fur and glittering teeth.

Rose and I have a rare moment of total agreement.

As the wolf at the front of the pack jumps forward we dive into the icy chute. We slam down and start to slide, our arms and legs tangled, our screams competing with the snarls of the wolves.

The tunnel becomes steeper. I wrap my arms round

Rose's legs and she grabs hold of my hair, and we don't let go. It's painful, and we can't protect our heads, but at least the wolves haven't followed us. The chute must be too steep. It drops away beneath us and in total darkness we slide round corners, twisting left, then right, all the time picking up speed. My foot hits a rock, sending a jolt of pain up my ankle, but I barely feel it because just then my head scrapes along a lump of ice.

We tumble over a lip of rock and then we're flying through the air. We land with a thump. My face is pressed into ice, but most of my fall has been broken by Rose, who is squashed underneath me.

She groans and mutters, 'Get off me, you lump!'

I stagger to my feet and despite the pain that's throbbing through every part of my body, my heart lifts. We're alive and we've lost the wolves! Their howls have faded away to nothing and now we are surrounded by a deep echoing silence.

'Conker bum!'

Ah, not quite silence. A spluttering blue flame pierces the blackness and I see Win's grinning face and his half-snapped wand. His nose is bleeding and he has a purple bruise on one cheek.

'That,' he says, pointing his wand at the hole we've just fallen through, 'was the coolest thing I've ever done in my life!'

He runs his floppy wand over us to check for damage.

'You're all right,' he says, prodding my cheek. 'Rose, you've going to have a black eye and you've got a cut on your chin, but basically you're both fine.'

'Well, we're not *really* fine,' I say. 'Presumably we're still being chased by wolves and that lunatic Hati Skoll, and we're lost inside an ice mountain.'

'*Presumably!*' says Rose, imitating me. 'Don't be so negative, Arthur. For one thing, how do you know we're lost?'

'Er, because we don't know where we are. Are we in a cave, or a tunnel? We haven't got a clue because our only light source is Win's teeny-weeny flame.'

Win does an outraged gasp and his flame flickers out. 'Your negativity has killed my magic!' he says.

'No, it hasn't,' I say. 'Your rubbish magic did that all on its own!'

For a moment none of us speak. We stand in the dark, listening to the *drip, drip, drip* of melting ice. I'm cold, my whole body hurts, and now I've got over the happiness of being alive, I'm starting to panic. Not only are we trapped in this mountain, but Crowky has got The Box. Then Rose says, 'You're being a massive idiot, Arthur,' and I realise she's right. The three of us sticking together is the only thing we've got going for us right now.

'I know, sorry,' I say. 'It's just a bit . . . claustrophobic in here.'

'You can say that again,' says Rose, and I remember that she hates the dark.

'We've got to stay calm,' I say. 'We've got to get out of this mountain and get to safety. I mean, *if* we can get out of here . . . Maybe we've fallen into a pit . . . Maybe there's no way out!'

'Arthur, that is not staying calm,' says Rose, then she takes a deep breath. 'First we need to see. If we can see, then we can work out where we are and what we need to do.' I hear her rummaging around in Mitch's bag. She whispers a word, there's a swooshing sound and a dazzling light appears. It's coming from a small bottle.

'What's that?' I say.

'Just a bit of M.O.O.N. magic,' says Rose. 'Penguin breath, starlight and squid ink. Mitch made it for me.' She shakes the bottle and it glows even brighter.

'It's not as good as conker bum,' mutters Win, 'but I suppose it will work.'

It will definitely work. I can see where we are now; we're in a round icy chamber, the opening of the chute is above us and another tunnel twists away into the darkness. It must lead somewhere!

Relief sweeps through me, and the others obviously feel it too because our aches and pains are forgotten as we start to run down the tunnel.

It's long and dark. Soon we find smaller tunnels leading off in all directions, but we stick to the main one and Rose's bottle shows us which way to go. As we jog along, listening carefully for padding paws and distant growls, I think about the fears that first came out of The Box.

'You know Candyfloss and Bendy Joan,' I say. 'Are you sure we didn't do something to make them go away?' Already I'm feeling tired and I'm wondering how long we're going to be able to keep running.

'It was so long ago,' Rose says. 'I can't remember.'

'I can remember what happened before Candyfloss went,' says Win. 'Arthur squeezed his nose!'

We stop for a rest. Rose holds up her bottle light and

I see her smile. 'Yes, you did, Arthur. It honked really loudly and Candyfloss was not expecting it. We never saw him again after that.'

I can just about picture this happening: Candyfloss's shocked expression, and how he walked off in a huff.

'And Rose, Bendy Joan went after you jumped out on her,' says Win. 'You sat in a tree waiting for the perfect moment, then – bang! – you pounced like a ninja.'

And then, even though we're exhausted and almost certainly being chased by wolves, Rose starts laughing. 'I got her real good!'

'You did,' says Win, slapping her on the shoulder. 'You took her to stealth school.'

Rose's laughing stops abruptly and she looks down the long dark tunnel. 'I don't think honking noses or jumping out of trees will work this time,' she says. 'Come on. We need to get out of here.'

We start to run again, the light bobbing along the walls of the tunnel. 'I really hope this tunnel leads somewhere,' I say.

'It might take us back to the Vampire,' says Win. 'Maybe Mitch will be waiting for us, and she'll have overpowered Crowky and got The Box back!'

Maybe, I think, but this tunnel really doesn't feel like it's leading us back to the Vampire. It feels like it's taking us deeper and deeper into the mountain.

CHAPTER 39

Just when we're thinking we can't run any further we see a blue light up ahead. Rose puts her bottle in her bag – we don't need it now – and we run towards it.

'We're coming out of the mountain!' shouts Win.

But when we burst out of the tunnel we realise we're still inside the mountain, in a vast chamber of ice. Passageways lead off in all directions and long, thick icicles hang over our heads. All around, ice glitters. It's beautiful and quite bizarre. Columns of sunlight beam down on us from holes high in the ceiling.

'It feels warm,' says Rose, turning in her own spotlight of sunshine.

'We'll be out of here soon,' I say, mainly to reassure myself. The mountain that saved us from the wolves has started to feel like a prison, but feeling the light on my skin has given me a rush of hope. 'Rose, have you still got that compass?'

We discover we've been running north so we decide

to keep going in that direction. North might be taking us further away from Mitch and the ship, but it's also taking us away from Hati and the wolves. The last thing we want to do is bump into them.

'This way,' says Win, pointing at a low tunnel at the opposite end of the chamber.

'Let's go,' I say, but Rose doesn't move.

She's still standing under her beam of light, only now she's frowning. 'Can you hear that?'

I listen. To begin with, all I can hear is the dripping of the icicles that surround us, but then I hear a scrabbling sound, and something else . . . panting. It seems to be coming from one of the tunnels.

I shake my head. These ice caves can do funny things to your mind, make you see and hear things that aren't really here. But then a long, sinister howl echoes around us.

'RUN!' shouts Rose, and we follow Win into the tunnel. We're plunged into darkness. Rose wrestles with her bag, then we hear the bottle clatter to the ground. We drop to our knees, feeling around on the cold floor. A volley of growls rings out behind us. The wolves must be in the chamber. It will only take them a few moments to discover which tunnel we're in.

'Got it!' says Win, and he thrusts it at Rose.

Moments later light fills the tunnel and we are off.

Rose gasps. 'We can't outrun them!'

'We have to try,' I say, forcing my legs to move faster, ignoring the pain in my chest and focusing on the padding footsteps that seem to be getting louder.

Then Win shouts, 'Up ahead . . . I can hear water!'

So can I. It's moving fast, rushing and tumbling.

The tunnel turns and opens out on a ledge of ice. We slide to a stop just in time. Our path is blocked by an underground river. It races past us, deep and wide and impossible to cross.

'What do we do?' says Rose. 'We're trapped!'

Her words are followed by howls and we turn to see the wolves pouring out of the tunnel. They creep towards us like one creature, heads low, teeth bared, their claws skittering on the ice. They surround us, pushing us closer and closer to the river. When we're teetering on the edge of the ice, our heels hanging over the water, they come to a stop. They wait, mouths hanging open, saliva dripping. One leaps at Rose, but a sharp whistle makes it slink back.

Hati is coming.

The wolves' eyes dart to the tunnel and then back to Rose. Their tails curl under. *They look like us*, I think. *They look scared.*

Hati Skoll strolls into the cave. She walks up to her wolves and rests her gloved hands on two huge heads. The brown leather disappears into their fur.

She sees Rose hiding between me and Win and grins. 'Caught you!' She sounds gleeful, like she's playing a game.

'Now you've got to join my pack.'

Rose shakes her head, but she doesn't answer back or shout. Normally my sister is the fierce one out of the two of us, but something about Hati makes her fall silent. I decide to speak for her. 'You'll have to take all three of us. Rose isn't going anywhere without me and Win.'

Hati scowls. 'No. I only want her.' She strokes the snout of an almost black wolf, the smallest in the pack. 'Flea is not a pup any more. I need a new runt.'

My sister, *a runt*? It seems ridiculous but next to me Rose is shrinking back, trying to make herself invisible.

And that's when I see something. A large chunk of ice is floating down the river. It spins for a moment before bouncing off a rock and drifting towards us.

Win's seen it too, but Hati is too busy staring at Rose to notice it.

I reach behind Rose and tug on Win's cloak. It's not much of a signal, but I'm hoping he'll understand that the piece of ice could rescue us.

'*Rose!*' shouts Hati. Instantly Rose looks up. 'Come here. *Now.*'

And I actually feel Rose move to step forward. It's like she's hypnotised by Hati's cold eyes and voice. I hold on tight to her sleeve. The flat piece of ice is drifting past us.

'Go!' I shout to Win, and he turns and leaps. He smacks down on the ice, his fingertips gripping the sides, his feet trailing in the dark water. His weight makes the ice spin a little closer to me and Rose.

'Rose, jump!' I shout, but she just stands there as if she's frozen to the ground, so I shove her and I see the look of shock on her face as she tumbles backwards, arms scrabbling at the air. She lands half in the water, but Win's already grabbed hold of her and is pulling her up next to him.

Now it's my turn. I start to run.

'Come on, Arthur!' Win shouts. The chunk of ice must have caught in a current because it's picking up speed. I run alongside them on the slippery ledge. I have to jump now before they disappear into the tunnel . . . but the gap has got wider. I can't make it!

I hear Hati's whistle and see a flash of black fur as Flea leaps after me.

I jump. I have no choice.

I fall into the freezing water. The shock is instant, like concrete slamming into my body. I can't breathe. I can't think. But then I feel hands grabbing my shoulders, pulling me out of the water. And something else. A jabbing pain in my ankle.

When I lift my face out of the water I see my foot clamped in Flea's jaw and her shoulders straining as she drags me back to shore. I kick out, as hard as I can. The pain eases, but still I'm being pulled towards the ledge, and I'm taking Rose and Win back with me. Flea has her teeth sunk into the leg of my fur onesie. She tosses her head from side to side, and my leg flies round in the air. My head is forced back under the water.

Hati walks towards us, taking her time, followed by the rest of the wolves.

I splutter to the surface. 'The wolf's got me,' I shout. 'Rose, Win, let go!' But when I glance back I see that it's just Rose holding on to my shoulders. Win, inexplicably, has taken off his onesie and is wriggling out of his trousers. I don't have time to think why he's doing this because while Flea pulls me closer to shore, I realise Rose is losing her grip. I reach out my hand and Rose grabs hold of it. Her fingers feel warm and strong . . . but not strong enough. My fingers are icy. *Twigs like Crowky's*, I think and then I realise that I no longer feel cold. In fact, I feel warm. This can't be a good thing.

'*Rose,*' I whisper, or maybe I just think it because everything has started to slow down and even the colour seems to have disappeared from my sister's face.

A coil of rope flies past me and lands on the ice between Rose and Win.

'Pull yourself in, Rose!' shouts Hati. 'Can't you see your brother is freezing?'

I try to shake my head, but my body won't work any more.

'Boggle hiss!' I only just hear Win's spell. Water washes over my face, but I see him waving his trousers over his head and pointing his wand. 'Boggle hiss.

BOGGLE HISS!' he yells.

An explosion of black stars fills the cave and my foot shoots free. Rose drags me out of the river and on to the lump of ice. Our raft bobs and spins towards the dark tunnel.

Back on the ledge Flea looks confused. Win's trousers dangle from her jaws and Win is now clutching my onesie.

Hati's eyes fill with rage. 'I'm going to hunt you down, Rose Trout!' she shouts as we slip into the darkness of the tunnel. 'You can *never* escape from me!'

CHAPTER 40

I lie on the ice, my teeth chattering and my body numb. I listen to Win talk about his magic and I enjoy the incredible sensation of being swept further and further away from Hati Skoll and her wolves.

'Did you see my trousers in the wolf's mouth?' he says. 'I did the switching hex and it worked even though my wand is broken! That's potent magic, guys, but I did it!' He's so delighted he wriggles around, making our raft tip. Water splashes over my already frozen feet.

As Win chatters on, I manage to work out that when Win did the spell my fur onesie instantly swapped places with his trousers. Rose has helped me back into my onesie, but it's soaking and, if anything, it's made me even colder. I lie back, shivering, and I listen to Win boast.

'I mean, I'm a bit cold now and I'm in my pants, but that's the best magic I've ever done in my life. I bet Mitch couldn't do it!'

I know I should say something, thank him for saving my life, but right now I'm too exhausted.

'Arthur's cold,' says Rose, giving me a prod. 'He's stopped talking.'

'Leave this to me,' says Win, his voice brimming with new-found confidence. Through half-frozen eyelashes I see him take out his broken wand and point it at me.

'Wait . . . ' I whisper, but he's already begun muttering, his eyes half-closed.

'MISTER FLAMBAYGO!' he booms, his voice echoing around us.

A golden bubble starts to grow out of the end of his wand. It looks like it's being slowly inflated. It lights up the tunnel we're floating through and I see that the ice ceiling isn't far above our heads. Water swirls around us and the sides of the tunnel are smooth. We couldn't get off this raft, even if we wanted to.

Still holding his wand and the golden light up high, Win leans close to me and whispers, 'The magical heat of Mister Flambaygo will warm you to the core, Arthur.' Then he wiggles the wand, making the ball teeter for a moment before dropping into my lap.

It's like a balloon of fire.

'Aaaagh!' I scream, jerking upright. I scoop up the burning sphere and toss it in the air. It lands on my shoulder, making me scream again, then it rolls down over me before coming to a stop in the middle of the raft.

For a second it sits there, then it melts a hole through the ice before disappearing into the water with a hiss.

'*Imaginary*,' whispers Win.

'And really, really, hot,' I say, pressing my burnt fingers down on the ice.

'Don't be so ungrateful, Arthur,' says Rose. 'Look, "Mister Flambaygo" even dried your onesie.'

She's right. There might be a scorch mark running across it, but it feels like it's just come out of a tumble dryer. For a moment I close my eyes and enjoy the incredible sensation of warm fluffy fur. Now I'm not cold I can start

to be grateful to Win. 'Nice magic, mate,' I say, clapping a hand on his shoulder.

'I know,' he says, nodding, 'and now we've also got a useful hole in the raft.'

Luckily the hole doesn't make the raft sink, but icy water does shoot through it every now and then.

It's creepy being in the dark surrounded by water but we decide not to use Mitch's magic bottle of light. We're not sure how long it will last and when we might need it. Instead we slip along in the pitch black and talk about how spectacularly badly our mission has gone.

'Crowky's got The Box,' says Rose, not that I needed reminding.

'We're being chased by an aggressive girl and her wolves,' I add.

'And we're on a chunk of ice floating along a river in a mountain and we don't know where we are!' Win adds gleefully. 'What an adventure . . .'

At that moment our raft bangs into something, spins round, then bashes against something else, and we decide it's time to use Mitch's magic bottle.

Rose gives it a shake and the bright light appears. Now we can see that the underground river has got wider and sharp rocks are sticking out of the water. The river is flowing too fast for us to stop moving, so all we can do is shift our weight from side to side to try and avoid the rocks. This works for a while, but soon there are just too many rocks and we start banging against them.

We huddle together in the middle of the raft, water sloshing through the hole, hoping we don't tip over. Then we spot a pink light glowing in the distance.

Rose puts the bottle away and the light becomes clearer. It might be tiny, but it's a brilliant sight because it looks like, finally, we're coming to the end of the tunnel. As we drift forward we start talking over each other as we wonder what we're going to find on the other side of the mountain.

'There might be a town full of wizards!' says Win.

'Or lizards,' I suggest.

'Or fairies,' says Rose. 'Remember my fairy game, Arthur? That's got to be here somewhere.'

I definitely sent Rose's fairies to The End after they appeared in Roar because they were really violent and scary. For a while Rose and I reminisce about the fairies, forgetting for a moment that Win is listening to us.

'I don't get it,' he says, interrupting us. 'Why would Rose's fairy game turn up in Roar?'

This throws Rose, but only for a second. 'Game is another of our words for magic, like "playing". What I'm saying is that I might have magicked fairies here.'

'Nice,' he says with a smile. 'I'd like to meet a fairy.'

'No you wouldn't,' I say. 'Rose's fairies bit, and they're weren't tiny things. They were normal sized, and they didn't even have wings.'

Perhaps it's all this talk of biting fairies, but something makes us fall quiet as we float towards the pink light.

Then Rose says, 'Can you two hear that?'

We can. It's coming from up ahead: an ominous crashing sound. 'Is it thunder?' I say, although that doesn't seem to go with the beautiful pink light.

'Maybe another river?' suggests Rose.

'Nah,' says Win. 'That's a waterfall.'

As soon as he says this we know that he's right. We cling to the ice, suddenly aware that while we've been chatting about fairies the raft has picked up speed. Now it's shooting straight towards the end of the tunnel. No, I correct myself, it's shooting straight towards the top of a waterfall.

Rose drops to her stomach and starts to paddle with her hands, trying to force the block of ice towards the rocks at the side. I help while Win does spells. But he's either panicking or his run of good magic has worn out because all he manages to do is fill the tunnel with coloured smoke.

'Slouchy fire!' he shouts. 'Whisper fly!'

'Win, stop it!' I yell. 'We can't see a thing!'

Our craft gets caught in a current and starts to spin round. Rose and I give up trying to paddle and Win stuffs his wand back in his onesie and we just hold on to each other. The edge of the waterfall is getting closer and closer. I think it's Win who starts screaming first, then Rose and I join in. At least, I think we're screaming. The thundering of the waterfall is so loud, it's all we can hear.

'This is it!' shouts Win as we reach the very edge. 'I LOVE YOU GUYS!'

And then our little raft, which has carried us safely through the mountain, slips between two rocks . . . and gets stuck.

We look at each other, wide-eyed, hardly daring to believe our luck.

'Still love you,' whispers Win.

'Don't move,' says Rose. She's closest to the mouth of the tunnel and is able to lean into the mist and peer down. She whips her head back in. 'It's a seriously big drop,' she says. 'It makes the On-Off Waterfall look like a leaky tap.

If we fall down there then we will definitely, you know, d—'

'Rose, we get it,' I say. 'Let's get off this thing before it melts.' Because I've noticed that the force of the water rushing past is shrinking our block of ice at an alarming rate.

'Good idea!' says Win, and before we can stop him he gets to his feet and leaps towards a rock.

Rose and I are immediately tossed forward and our faces plunge through the mist. I get a brief glimpse of a terrifying drop, and rocks, and certain death, before Win slams his foot down on the block of ice, making us fall back inside the cave.

We cling to each other, as Win laughs and says, 'Looks like I saved your life *again*!' Rose and I stare at him. '*What?*' he protests. 'I did!'

'Win, just keep your foot on there until we've got off,' says Rose through gritted teeth.

We're now squished together on the block of ice. We have a quick discussion about who should get off first and agree to jump off at exactly the same time, aiming for different rocks.

'On the count of three,' says Rose as we climb to our feet, the ice wobbling beneath us. 'One . . . two . . .'

'THREE!' yells Win. Rose throws herself off the ice a second before me and I'm pitched forward again. There is this moment where I fly out over the waterfall, catching my second glimpse of certain death, before Win pulls me back to safety.

'Saved you *again*!' he says with a happy chuckle.

My legs are wobbling so much that Win has to help me to the side of the river. We use the rocks as stepping stones until we reach a flat ledge.

The mist of the waterfall still forms a barrier blocking our view. 'Ready to see what's on the other side of the mountain?' says Rose.

Then together we step through the mist.

I shade my eyes against the setting sun. This is what made the light so pink. We're standing at the top of a waterfall surrounded by forest. The branches of frozen trees dip in the thundering water as it crashes down into a pool. Beyond the pool is a snowy plain. Animal tracks criss-cross the glittering snow and in the distance I can see a village clinging to the coast.

But it's what lies beyond all this that makes us stand so still and silent.

The ocean surrounding the village is covered in icebergs and floes, but further out the sea is blue and I can see islands stretching to the horizon. These aren't small rocky islands like the ones in the Archie Playgo – they're huge and lush and green.

'What's on those islands?' I say.

Rose smiles. 'I don't know, but we got it all wrong, didn't we? This isn't The End at all. It's just the beginning!'

CHAPTER 41

'That's where we've got to go.' I point at the village on the coast. It's made up of wooden buildings, some built on stilts over the sea, which stand silhouetted against the setting sun. The village looks ramshackle, and possibly abandoned, but it's got to be warmer than where we are right now. Night is coming and a freezing wind has started to blow off the waterfall. We need to get to shelter.

Rose nods, her teeth chattering, and Win pulls out his telescope. 'We'll find the warmest building and make a fire,' he says.

'And find some food,' I say. Suddenly I'm starving.

'And wash it down with a lovely pint of hot muskot glögg,' adds Win, smacking his lips.

'What's *that*?' says Rose.

Win shrugs, still gazing through the telescope. 'I don't know, but they sell it at The Bucket of Blood.'

He passes me the telescope and I scan across the snowy landscape until I find the little village. One of the buildings

227

is bigger than the others: a wooden tower that's built on stilts. A sign hangs over a door with the words 'The Bucket of Blood' written across it in red paint. I shift the telescope and see that Win's right. HOT MUSKOT GLÖGG is advertised on the side of the building.

I don't know what hot muskot glögg is, but right now I want some more than anything in the world. 'Let's go,' I say, shoving the telescope in my pocket.

Rose leads us away from the waterfall and down a track that winds through the forest. 'We need to be quick,' she calls over her shoulder. 'The sun's setting.'

She doesn't mention Hati Skoll and the wolves, or Crowky and The Box, but I'm sure that's what drives us on through the silent, deserted forest. A crow bursts from the branches of a tree, making us jump, and then a mournful wail whistles through the trees.

'Just the wind,' says Win, and we carry on trudging through the thick snow.

Night falls as we cross the plain, but we don't need to use Mitch's bottle to see where we're going. The full moon lights our way, making the snow sparkle and giving us the shadows of giants.

We walk in silence, our breath misting the air, until, finally, we reach a path. Ahead of us comes the distant suck and crash of waves. 'We're getting close,' says Rose, 'and look.' She's spotted a wooden signpost. We brush away snow to reveal messy writing.

'BaRRaCuda BaY,' Win reads. 'What's that?'

Rose lets out a sigh of exasperation. 'I'll tell you what *Barracuda Bay* is, Win. It's Arthur's stupid pirate village and it was always full of endless sword fights with monkey pirates who went around going, "oooh arrr!", and now we've got to sleep in it!'

'It wasn't stupid. It was awesome,' I mutter, as we turn and walk on towards the village. Barracuda Bay was part of the pirate game I was always trying to get Rose to play in Grandad's attic. I don't remember the village ever appearing in Roar. I guess Rose sent it packing to The End the moment she saw it.

'At least we've got somewhere to sleep,' I say. The path is leading us closer to the small houses with their shuttered windows. 'And I can't see any lights or smoke coming from chimneys. You don't need to worry about monkey sword fights, Rose. This place is deserted.'

'I can see a light,' says Win, pointing at a tall building. A creaking sign swings above a battered door. It's the inn we saw through his telescope.

I shiver. 'I wonder who lit the lamp?'

'Let's find out,' says Win, and doing his very best stealth walk he leads us through the silent village until we're standing outside The Bucket of Blood.

The inn is built over the sea on thick wooden posts. The whole building leans to one side and it looks like each floor has been added on as an afterthought. Planks are hammered on top of each other, the windows are wonky and the shutters look like they've been made out of old crates.

'You go first,' says Rose, nudging me forward. 'After all, this is your creation.'

She's right, and even though I've never actually been here, little details – the red dripping letters on the sign, the rum barrels stacked against the door – feel familiar. If I had to imagine a sinister inn in a frozen pirate

village, this is definitely the kind of thing I would come up with.

I reach for the door, then hesitate. Should I bang on the brass knocker or walk right in? *Walk right in*, I decide, lifting the heavy latch, because that's what a pirate would do.

The door opens with a creak and we shuffle into a dimly lit room. It smells of fish and old beer. A couple of candles flicker on the bar, and the planks below our feet are spaced so wide I can see slivers of dark sea swirling below us. But the important thing is, it's warm. A fire burns in the corner of the room. I run to it and stretch my hands towards the glowing coals.

'It's going to be OK,' I say, to reassure myself. 'We're going to be OK!'

'Erm, Arthur?' Win's voice is surprisingly high.

'What?' I shove my fingers close to the fire.

'There's a bear watching you and she's got a whopping big cutlass!'

CHAPTER 42

I spin round. Of course someone's in the Bucket of Blood. Who else lit the fire?

The bear is sitting on a stool behind the door, the cutlass resting on her lap. Her teeth are bared and her eyes are round and staring. Scars cover her patchy fur and a gold hoop dangles from one ear. Rather unusually for a bear she's wearing a dress covered in rosebuds with a filthy apron tied over the top.

Rose gasps and says, '*Carol Brocklebank?*' The bear nods and Rose turns to glare at me. 'Arthur, did you put my Sylvanian bear in your stupid pirate village?'

I shrug. 'I guess so,' I say, although, honestly, I can't remember.

'Rose . . . Arthur,' says Win, 'I don't know what you're talking about, but that bear looks angry!'

'*Arrrrrggghhh!*' growls Carol. Then she hops off the stool, ducks under the bar and reappears a moment later. She raises a dirty clawed finger and beckons me closer.

'Who? Me?' I say, but Rose is already pushing me forward.

Carol runs the tip of her sabre over the bottles behind the bar, making them clink. Then she looks at me and raises a bushy eyebrow.

'She wants to know what we're having to drink,' says Rose.

Win bangs his fist on the bar. 'Hot glögg!'

It seems like the safest choice. 'Three pints of hot muskot glögg, please,' I say to the bear.

She nods, like I've made an excellent choice, then lifts the lid off a steaming cauldron and ladles something thick and brown into mugs. Then she holds out a paw.

Win nudges me. 'Go on, Arthur, pay her.'

I feel in my pockets, but except for the map, they're empty. 'I haven't got anything to pay her with. Give her the light bottle, Rose, or the compass.'

'No!' Rose clutches Mitch's bag to her. 'We must have something else she'd like. What would you have paid with when you were little?'

'I don't know. Leaves . . . stones? Imaginary money?'

'Try that,' she says.

Feeling a bit stupid I pull a handful of invisible coins out of my pocket. 'One,' I say and I mime dropping the coin into her paw, 'two, three.'

The bear stares at her paw and scowls.

'Don't be so stingy,' says Rose. 'Give her more.'

So I drop the whole handful of invisible coins into her paw and even pick one up that's rolled on to the floor. The bear nods, satisfied, and we take our brimming mugs over to a table by the fire.

The drink tastes a bit like hot-cross buns and it gives me a warm glow inside. For a while we sip in silence, then the bear picks up an accordion and starts to play a sinister tune.

'Really one of us should be on watch,' says Rose. 'When Hati and the wolves get out of the mountain they're going to come straight across the plain. If we know they're coming we'll have time to escape.'

'We can't keep running away,' I say. 'We're heading further and further away from Home. We've got to stop sometime.'

'You can stop,' says Rose, wrapping her hands round her mug. 'I'm going to keep on going until I get away from them, or they go away.'

'But, Rose, what if you can't run away from them?' I say. 'I honked Candyfloss's nose and you jumped out on Bendy Joan before they went. Maybe you've got to do something to Hati and the wolves to get rid of them.'

'In case you hadn't noticed, Arthur, six massive wolves are chasing me. What could I possibly do to get rid of them?'

Rose glares at me as Carol's sinister music plays in the background.

'You got rid of the Dark,' says Win. The Dark was this

big black cloud that followed Rose wherever she went and kept trying to wrap itself around her. 'I can remember exactly what you did before it went away.'

Rose looks at him curiously. 'What did I do?'

'You ran into the middle of it,' says Win, his eyes shining bright with the memory, 'and you danced in it, and you were laughing like mad. You got us to join in too. Remember?'

'I do,' she says, smiling. 'I called it the Dark Disco.'

'*You were laughing like mad . . .*' I repeat Win's words.

'So what?' says Rose.

'Maybe that's it. It was funny when I honked Candyfloss's nose, *and* when you jumped out on Bendy Joan. I bet we were laughing then too.'

Rose looks at me. 'So you think I should go up to the wolves and laugh? That's not going to work, Arthur!'

'Fine,' I say. 'They're your fear; what do *you* think will work?'

'How many times do I have to tell you?' she says, standing up and banging down her mug. 'They're *not* my fear. I like wolves and Hati Skoll is just a girl who wears way too many stupid tassels.' And with that she stomps out of the inn.

Win eyes her abandoned drink. 'Do you think she's finished with that?'

I shrug. Right now, I haven't got a clue what Rose is thinking.

Outside, I can see Rose standing in the empty street, her eyes fixed on the path that leads out of the village. Rose can make all the jokes about tassels that she wants, but I know she's lying. I saw how she changed when Hati got out of The Box; I felt her trembling next to me. She's not scared of Hati. She's terrified of her.

CHAPTER 43

Cold and hunger soon drive Rose back inside. She shakes the snow off her onesie and says, 'Do you reckon Carol Brocklebank does food?'

It turns out Carol does do food, but it's not the usual pub menu of pies and scampi. Instead she serves two things: stew and ship's biscuit, and stew and no ship's biscuit.

The food comes in wooden bowls and it's hot and filling; I can't imagine anything tasting better, not even scampi and chips. Before we've finished, the bear decides her day's work is over. She wipes our crumbs on to the floor with a filthy rag then drops a key on the table. 'Arrgghh!' she says as she stomps up a rickety staircase.

Rose picks up the key and we take the remaining stub of candle and go upstairs to investigate. The key opens the first door we come to.

Moonlight streams into a room, revealing one bed with a dirty blanket, two windows – one facing the sea, the other the mountains – a small fireplace, a hammock strung from the ceiling and a stuffed parrot.

'How very piratical,' says Rose, running a finger through the thick dust on the parrot's beak. 'I'm so glad we didn't end up at my fairy kingdom with its cosy tree dwellings and magical fairies.'

'Who bit,' I remind her.

'Well at least there's a fire,' says Win and he tries to use Mister Flambaygo to bring it to life. When this and several other spells don't work, I suggest he tries the candle and the wood catches immediately. 'My magic must have warmed it up,' he says cheerfully.

Rose looks out of the window that faces the mountains and announces that it's perfect for keeping watch. She's right. From here we can see right across the plain; there's no way Hati and the wolves will be able to sneak up on us.

While Rose lies on the bed staring up at the ceiling, Win fiddles with the fire and I investigate a hatch in the floor. When I pull it open a blast of cold air hits me and I'm surprised to see that I'm staring down at the sea. It looks particularly inky and deep. Chunks of ice knock against the wooden posts holding up the Bucket of Blood, and there's something else down there too. At first I think it's a boat, but then I see a cracked beak and two large eyes, and I realise that it's a swan pedalo.

I decide not to mention it to Rose. The pedalo is covered in green algae and it looks ancient; I don't want her to suggest we set off in it right now. Still, it feels good to know we've got an escape hatch and a getaway vehicle.

I let the hatch slam shut, and when I turn round I see that Rose has curled up and fallen asleep. Just looking at her makes me yawn, so when Win offers to take first watch I don't argue. I stumble into the hammock and snuggle into my onesie. 'Wake me for the second watch,' I mutter, before adding, 'and, Win, make sure you don't fall asleep.'

I don't drift off straight away. I think about Crowky and The Box, and how he must be hunting for us. Then I think about Rose dancing in the Dark Disco, her head thrown back, laughing at the top of her voice. Can our laughter really make the fears vanish?

I puzzle this over, my hammock sways and the fire crackles. And then, in the way that often happens just as you're drifting off to sleep, the pieces of the puzzle fall into place. What if it wasn't the laughter that made our fears go away, but the fact that we *could* laugh? You can't really, truly laugh at something you're scared of.

When we stop feeling scared, the fear goes away . . .

Could it really be that simple? I wonder as I slip into a sleep that's as deep and quiet as the sea that's swirling below us.

CHAPTER 44

A long deep growl creeps into my dreams. It runs down my spine and makes the hairs on my arms stand on end. I hear it again, and I realise that I'm not asleep, and that the growling is coming from somewhere near my face. Then I feel hot breath panting on me and I smell something disgusting.

With my stomach clenched tight with fear, I open my eyes.

A wolf is centimetres away from my face. It has eyes the colour of dirty snow, and when it growls I see wet gums and stained teeth. A jaunty whistle makes the wolf slink back. Hati Skoll is standing in the middle of the room.

'Hello, Arthur Trout,' she says, peering at me from under her hat.

I sit up. The window has been thrown open, letting in freezing air and the odd snowflake. The door is open too, and wet footprints are dotted across the floor. Two more wolves prowl around the room. Rose is standing pressed against the wall, trying to get as far away from them as possible and Win is tied to a chair. He struggles from side to side, and makes a grunting sound. He's got something stuffed in his mouth. There's another chair behind his, and I know it's for me.

Seeing my shocked face Hati grins and says, 'My wolves can be very, very quiet when they need to be.'

I look at Win. 'You fell asleep?' I say. I can't believe it. We managed to survive the tunnels in the mountain, being chased by wolves, the underground river *and* a freezing trek through the snow. And then Win *fell asleep*.

He stops struggling and looks at me with big eyes. Then he nods.

Hati laughs. 'And we just strolled in and found you waiting for us. I enjoyed the chase, but the end was far too easy. You didn't even lock the door!' She gives the empty chair a kick. 'Sit here.'

I remember the last thought I had before I fell asleep, and I decide there's no way I'm going to let Hati Skoll think I'm scared of her.

'No,' I say.

Hati lurches forward and grabs hold of me. 'You've not got it, have you, Arthur? *Everyone* does what I say!' Then she whistles and the wolf guarding me bites the front of my onesie. Together they tug me out of the hammock. I crash to the floor and I'm dragged to the chair, shouting and kicking. Hati yanks my hands behind my back and ties

them together. For good measure, she slings a rope round
me and Win and pulls it tight.

The only thing left free are my legs. I'm about to start
banging them up and down, but something stops me.
Perhaps it's the realisation that if I keep fighting I'm going
to end up with something stuffed in my mouth like Win,
and then I won't be able to speak to Rose.

Hati walks around the room, opening drawers and
poking the stuffed parrot. She picks up Mitch's bag and
shakes it upside down. Everything Rose has collected rolls
over the floor: some ink from Mitch's tattoo kit, the bottle
light, a shell necklace, a shrivelled apple. Hati sends the
ink flying with her foot, then steps on the necklace,
crushing the shells.

Then, like a child who suddenly realises how much fun it is to break stuff, she starts stamping on everything. The apple is mashed into the floor, the compass is crushed, and a pot of ink is cracked open. While she does this I try to get Rose's attention, but she's staring at the floor, flinching with each stamp of Hati's foot.

Hati abandons her game when she sees something out of the window. 'We're going,' she announces.

'Going?' I say. 'Where?'

She shrugs. 'I don't know, but I've spotted a ship and I've always wanted to take a long trip somewhere. I'm going to hunt at sea.' She walks over to Rose and stands too close to her. 'And you are coming with me!'

Rose shakes her head.

Hati imitates her, making her eyes go wide and shaking her head, then she bursts out laughing. She's got a loud laugh. The wolves join in too, barking excitedly, and Rose shrinks even further back.

'Rose!' I shout. 'Listen to me. I think I know how to get rid of her.' Hati spins round. 'Show her you're not scared. Say something . . . *anything*! Tell her what you think about her tassels!'

Hati crosses the room and stuffs a filthy scarf in my mouth. I can't talk. I can't even close my mouth and swallow. Satisfied, Hati goes back to Rose. 'What *do* you think of my tassels, Rose?'

'Nothing,' says Rose.

'Tell me.'

'I said they were . . . stupid.'

'*You're* stupid,' says Hati, poking her in the forehead. 'Now join the rest of my pack.'

I try to speak, but I can't. Rose walks towards the door.

'Stop!' shouts Hati. Rose stops. Hati clicks her fingers at her wolves. 'Mouse, Worm, Weed, get out.' The three wolves slink out of the room, snapping at Rose's hands and ankles as they go past. 'Now it's your turn, *Fish*.' Hati pushes Rose forward. 'How do you like your new name?'

I bang my feet up and down on the floor and try to scream, but Rose walks out of the door without looking back.

Hati picks up Win's telescope and trains it on the distant mountains. 'Guess who I can see?' she says. 'I'll give you a clue. He's made of straw, he's got wings and he's carrying a great big box.' She grins. 'I'd love to stick around and watch, but it's time for me to take your runt of a sister far, far away from here.' And with that she snaps the telescope shut, tosses it on the bed and clomps out of the room, her stupid tassels swinging.

CHAPTER 45

I try to push the gag out of my mouth and I pull at the ropes. Behind me, Win does the same. While I struggle, I stare out of the window. Even without the telescope I can see Crowky and his scarecrows. They're at the foot of the mountain and they form a dark shape that's heading our way.

I feel sick. Cold. But it's not because of Crowky or The Box, or even the snow that's blowing across my face. It's because of what Hati said. She called Rose *Fish*. I've heard one other person call Rose *Fish* and that's Harriet Scott back in Home. Could it be a coincidence? After all, Hati gives her wolves names that are meant to make them feel small . . .

No. A horrible feeling inside tells me it's more than that.

Hati . . . Harriet. It's not just their names that are similar. Hati loved smashing Rose's things; it was written all over her face as she crushed the glass bottle and stamped on

Rose's precious necklace. I remember how Rose's cupcakes were thrown all over the corridor at school. When I went looking for Rose I saw Harriet walking towards me and grinning . . . and she was surrounded by her pack of girls.

Finally I work the gag out of my mouth and take a deep breath. As I continue to struggle with the ropes, my mind jumps backward and forward between Hati and Harriet, looking for connections.

Behind me, Win gasps. He's got rid of his gag too. 'Arthur, I'm sorry I fell asleep,' he says in a rush. 'I didn't mean to. I was so tired!'

'It doesn't matter,' I say, because we really don't have time to talk about this right now. 'We've got to get out of here and get to Rose before they board the ship.'

'Oh no . . .' says Win.

I twist round, trying to see what he can see. 'What is it?'

'The ship . . . It's leaving!'

Frustration sweeps through me. Crowky is coming towards me, Rose is sailing away from me, and I'm stuck here, tied to the person who made this happen. No. That's not fair. Win didn't mean to fall asleep or let go of the map back at the Crow's Nest, but as he chatters on about the speed of the ship, and strength of the wind, and says, 'What do you think is in The Box, Arthur? Vampires? Or just one really massive snake?' I start to feel angry.

'Win, please, just . . . shut up,' I say, and instantly

he falls quiet.

'I can do that,' he says. 'Right now. I'm going to shut up and be totally silent . . . I'm not going to make a single sound.'

I struggle madly, trying to loosen the ropes. Suddenly I fall forward. The rope is undone. 'I did it, Arthur!' cries Win. 'I got us out!' The next thing I know my wrists and hands are free too.

Win jumps up, grabs his telescope and runs to the window facing land. 'I reckon Crowky is half an hour away,' he says. 'The scarecrows are marching and Crowky is doing that creepy flying-running thing he does. He is *itching* to get here.' He turns to look at me. 'What are we going to do, Arthur?'

My eyes dart between the two windows; I see the scarecrows moving across the plain and the ship sailing away with Rose on board. My throat feels tight and I've got a hot feeling in my chest. I swallow and try to think logically, but I can't. I'm too angry . . . I'm too scared. 'I don't know, Win.'

He pats my shoulder. 'At least the situation can't get any worse.'

With a crash, the trapdoor in the corner of the room flies open. I see a flash of bright blue as Mitch heaves herself into the room, banging her tail down with a wet thud. Her neck is loaded with bottles and amulets and her eyes are wild. When she sees it's just the two of us, she shouts,

'What have you done with Rose?'

'Hati took her,' I say.

She stares at me in disbelief. 'And you two are just standing here?'

'She tied us up and took

Rose away on a massive ship!' protests Win. 'What were we supposed to do?'

Mitch turns towards the window. 'That's MY massive ship!' she bellows, then looks at me and Win and she actually growls.

Win edges closer to me. 'Arthur, the situation *did* get worse!'

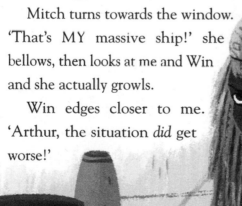

While Mitch brainstorms a plan of action, Win stares through the telescope and gives us a running commentary on Crowky's progress.

'He's so close I can actually see the straw flying off him!' he says.

Mitch drums her webbed fingers on the floorboards. 'I'll swim straight after the *Alisha*,' she says, 'sneak on board, grab Rose and bring her back.'

'But you can't swim back with Rose,' I say. 'She's not like you. She'll freeze in the water!'

Mitch's face lights up. 'I saw this boat-swan thingy. I'll take that.'

Just then Win gasps. 'Crowky is FLYING, Arthur! Nope. He's down again.'

I shake my head and try to ignore Win and focus on what Mitch is saying. 'Look, even if you do manage to get Rose off the boat, it won't help. Rose can't run away from Hati Skoll if she's going to get rid of her, she's got to stand up to her.'

Mitch groans with frustration. 'How do we get Rose to do that? And why didn't she do it the moment Hati Skoll climbed out of The Box? Hati's a girl. Rose controls dragons!'

'We've not got long until they are here,' says Win. 'Do you think it will be your fear coming out of The Box, Arthur?'

I take a deep breath, and try to push down the panic I'm feeling. But it's as out of control as the situation we're in. I know I should be worrying about The Box, but right now all I can think about is the fact that Rose is gone and unless I can speak to her she might never come back.

'Mitch, I think I know what to say to Rose, but you'll have to get me to her. Can you do that?'

Mitch frowns. 'Maybe . . . Give me a minute to think.'

Win thrusts the telescope into my hands. 'You've got to see this.'

I lift the telescope and run it over the plain. Suddenly Crowky's face appears – wild, excited, straw hair flying behind him. Clutched in front of him is The Box. My hands tighten on the telescope. 'Mitch,' I say, 'maybe we should *hide* while you do your thinking.'

She slams her tail on the floorboards, making the room shake. 'I have never hidden from anyone in my life, and I'm not about to start doing it because a scarecrow wants to open a box in front of you!'

'I get that,' I say, 'but it's not *your* fear that could come leaping out of The Box, is it? And if my fear does come out then I won't get to the *Alisha* in time and Rose will be GONE!'

Mitch reaches forward, grabs me by my onesie and pulls me close. 'Calm down, Arthur Trout, because I need to go foraging.'

'*Foraging?*' I don't believe this.

'Yes, *foraging*, I have to find some ingredients so I can make a fog spell that will hide the swan-thingy from my magnificently armed warship, making sure you don't get blown to pieces by a cannon – GOT IT?' I nod. 'Good. And that means I need you, Arthur Trout, Master of Roar, not to hide, but to buy me a bit of time. Create a distraction, fight those scarecrows, basically do anything that will let me find three sea urchins, a strand of toadflax, a pinch of starfish spit and seven grains of rice. Do you think you can do that?'

I swallow. 'Yes.'

'Good!' She lets go of my onesie and I stumble backwards. 'I'll let you know when I'm ready.'

'How?'

She runs her fingers through the vials round her neck then pulls one out. 'With a rainbow,' she says. Then she rolls across the floor, flops through the open trapdoor and lands in the sea with a splash.

I turn to Win. 'You heard her. We've got to create a

distraction or fight them off . . . any ideas?'

'We need weapons. What have we got to work with?'

We go to the window. Barracuda Bay looks even more desolate this morning than it did last night: the Bucket of Blood sign creaks in the wind and flurries of snow blow down the street. In the distance I can see Crowky and his army. Soon they will reach the path that leads to the village.

Win's eyes light up. 'I know what we've got tons of – snow! We can have a massive snowball fight!'

'Isn't snow a bit soft?' I say, thinking of the scarecrows' iron strength and Crowky's energy-sapping hands.

Win nods. 'Very, but I literally have no other ideas at all.'

Neither do I. 'A snowball fight it is,' I say, hoping Mitch does her foraging really, really quickly.

'YESSS!' shouts Win, and we turn and run down the rickety wooden stairs and through the bar.

'Morning, Carol!' says Win cheerfully.

The bear scowls and continues wiping a cloth round a smeared glass. I'd assumed Hati must have tied her up or locked her away somewhere, but I get the feeling she's been down here the whole time. It just goes to show that all pirates, even ones called Carol who wear flowery dresses, are totally untrustworthy.

CHAPTER 47

Outside the air is so cold it's like breathing ice, but we don't hesitate. We run to the edge of the village and duck down below a low wall. Then we start gathering snow and patting it into balls.

We stack them on the wall, working as fast as we possibly can. *Better than nothing*, I keep telling myself, all the time glancing up in the sky, looking out for Mitch's rainbow. I imagine the golden letters appearing on The Box and Crowky's hand reaching to open it, then SPLAT! He gets a snowball in the face. It could work, maybe, and this thought is enough to keep me scooping up handfuls of snow.

Soon we have a decent collection of snowballs and when we peer over the wall we see Crowky is a few minutes away. That's when Win comes up with the idea of doing his hanky paws spell.

'It's nothing special,' he admits, 'but it works every time. Basically it gives things a nice crust. I usually use it on toast or marshmallows but I reckon it would work on snow.'

We agree that he should do a test and he places one snowball on an abandoned cart.

'Hanky paws!' he says, thrusting his wand forward. Purple smoke pours from the wand and the snowball trembles then falls still. He runs forward and picks it up.

'Did it work?' I say.

'Let's see.' He turns and chucks it straight at me.

It's like a rock smacking me on the cheek. 'Yeah . . . It worked,' I say, rubbing my face.

Win gleefully starts hanky paws-ing every snowball we've made and soon a thick purple smog hangs over the entrance to the village. It's bright, but at least it hides us from view and we'll be able to launch a surprise attack on Crowky.

Then I spot the old cart and I have an idea. One end rests on the ground so that the bed forms a slope . . . a slope that leads directly towards the path that Crowky and his scarecrows are coming along.

Instead of adding the snowball in my hands to the pile, I roll it along the ground. It quickly picks up more snow, and I pack it down until it's as big as a football.

'Arthur, what are you doing?' says Win.

'I'm making a surprise for Crowky,' I say, then I explain my plan, all the time glancing back to the shore, looking for any sign of the rainbow.

'That's brilliant,' declares Win, and together we roll the

snowball round and round until we've got a great fat ball.

I look at the sloping bed of the cart. 'If we make it any bigger, we won't be able to push it into place.'

Win peers over the wall and through the thinning smoke. 'We need to get it up there right now,' he whispers. 'They're close.'

I look towards the shore: still no rainbow. 'Let's do it.'

We push the giant snowball up on to the cart. It's gigantic, massive, but there's just one problem: now we've got it up on the cart, we can't move. As we struggle to hold it in position, Win looks at me with a grin. 'I know this is scary, Arthur, and that Rose has gone, and that something bad might be waiting for you in The Box, but I can't wait to see this baby fly. It's going to be like bowling scarecrows!'

'That's the plan,' I say, keeping my eyes glued on the figures moving towards us. We can see them, but I don't think they can see us. The smoke has cleared now, but our onesies are white and it's begun to snow. We're camouflaged. Even so, I feel exposed as we stand by the cart, our arms quivering under the weight of the snowball.

'They're nearly here,' I whisper, and Win gets out his wand, ready to do the *hanky paws* spell.

Crowky is at the head of the pack. He's leaping forward, half running, half flying. The only thing slowing him down is The Box. It's big and it slips and slides in his hands. His scarecrow army jog behind him, trying to keep up.

Snow sticks to my eyelashes and face, but I don't move.

When Crowky reaches the signpost to the village, he stops and looks around. His button eyes move slowly from left to right, then they settle on us. . . I hold my breath.

'Now?' whispers Win, wand ready.

I shake my head because Crowky's eyes are moving again. The snow and our fur onesies have made us invisible. He hoists The Box in front of his face, and strides straight towards us. He's in the perfect position.

'Now?' asks Win.

'No,' I whisper. 'We need him to be close so he can't jump out of the way.'

Win's eyes widen. 'Got it! But I'll do the spell now so the snowball is rock hard and ready to go.'

'No, Win, the smoke!'

But already he's tapping his wand and hissing, 'Hanky paws!'

A puff of bright purple smoke billows around our faces and the snowball trembles. Crowky looks up and a smile creeps over his face. He puts The Box on the ground. 'I spy Arthur Trout!' he cries.

Win gasps. 'I'm sorry, Arthur!'

'Just . . . don't say or do anything else,' I say.

Crowky's eyes are fixed on the snowball. If we let it go now he'll just grab The Box, open his wings and swoop out of the way.

His twig fingers rest on the lid. 'Come on . . .' he snarls, eyes flicking to the side of The Box. He's willing the message to appear. '*Come on!*'

There's no point running. Crowky would just catch me and then I'll never get to Rose. This giant snowball is my only hope. I just need Crowky to be distracted.

Suddenly a golden light gleams on the side of The Box. It's happening. It knows I'm close. Crowky's eyes widen and he grins. 'I've got a feeling it's your turn, Arthur Trout!' he says, staring intently at the light.

This is the moment I've been waiting for.

'NOW!' I shout.

We let go of the snowball and it shoots down the sloping cart, along the path and straight towards Crowky. He looks up, and instinctively his wings open. He's about to fly up in the air when he remembers The Box. He reaches for it, but he's out of time. The snowball smacks into him and there is an explosion of straw and feathers. The Box flies to one side as Crowky is caught in the snowball and rolled round and round. He knocks into his scarecrows, scattering them in all directions, and keeps rolling down the hill until he hits a rock. The snowball collapses and for a moment Crowky just lies there, his wings sticking out at strange angles.

I look up in the air. What's Mitch doing? We need that rainbow!

Shaking snow from his body, Crowky jumps to his feet and utters a scream of rage. His scarecrows pick themselves up and start running towards us, but Crowky goes for The

Box. The light is still there, shining bright, pulsing, and now the letters have started to appear.

'Arthur!' shouts Win. 'Snowballs!'

We grab the snowballs and throw them. Win focuses on the scarecrow army, while I aim for Crowky. I get him on the shoulder and he staggers to the side. My next snowball misses, but my third hits him in the face, knocking him to the ground. But it's no good: immediately he's up and on his feet, sprinting towards The Box.

And then coloured light washes over us as the most magnificent rainbow I've ever seen bursts across the sky. The snowy plain turns into a patchwork of colour. It falls over me, Crowky and The Box.

Everyone stops to look, even Crowky.

I grab Win. 'GO!' I yell, and we turn and run towards the waiting pedalo.

CHAPTER 48

We're nearly at the shore, steps away from Mitch and the pedalo, when I feel the scrape of twig fingers on the back of my neck.

'Jump!' yells Mitch.

Win and I leap in the air and crash down in the pedalo. Mitch tosses something white and sparkly in the air then dives under the water and starts swimming. She's holding a rope and she's going so fast that Win and I are thrown to the back of the pedalo. Blood pounds in my ears as icy water splashes over me. Then I scramble up and look at Barracuda Bay.

Already Mitch's spell is working. A thick fog billows across the sea, hugging the shore and rising around the scarecrow army. Their ragged clothes blow in the wind and their eyes glitter as they stare after us. Crowky pushes his way through them, The Box clutched to his chest. The golden letters have disappeared. The look of rage on his face tells me that I got away just in time.

The distance between us grows and the fog becomes thicker, until Crowky and the scarecrows disappear from sight.

Win and I pick ourselves up from the bottom of the boat and sit on the fibreglass seat. I flop forward and I laugh, because I'm so exhausted and so amazed that we got away from Crowky.

'Where's the *Alisha*?' says Win.

I pull the telescope out of Mitch's bag and train it on the horizon. The fog is still spreading around us, but it hasn't reached the *Alisha* yet and I can see the ship racing out to sea. I track its progress. I'm not sure if it's my imagination, but the distance between us seems to be growing. Then the fog thickens and I lose sight of them.

We start to slow down and Mitch bursts out of the water. She leans on the side of the pedalo, dripping water over me and Win.

'It's no good,' she says. 'We can't catch up with them. I can't swim fast enough.'

Tendrils of fog swirl around us and I notice that frost has crept over Mitch's eyelashes and hair. It even dusts her brown tattooed arms, turning them a silvery grey. 'What can we do?' I ask. 'Can we help paddle or something?'

Mitch dismisses my suggestion with a wave of her hand. 'No. We need magic.'

'Yes!' says Win, pulling out his wand.

'Put it away,' says Mitch, picking through the bottles hanging round her neck. 'Marshmallows won't help us here.' She finds the bottle she's looking for and tugs out the cork. 'To be honest I wanted to save this for emergencies – like this pile of junk springing a leak – but I guess this is an emergency.' Her voice is even throatier than usual, a ragged whisper.

'Are you all right, Mitch?' I say. 'Is the water too cold for you?'

'Too cold? *Ha!*' she says, but her teeth are chattering and her fingers shake as she pours the contents of the bottle on to the frilled edges of her tail. Immediately the liquid turns bright blue and starts to fizz. 'Ooh . . . *ow!* That's a bit cold,' she admits with a sheepish smile.

'What does it do?' asks Win.

'It freezes stuff,' she says, then she slaps her tail down into the water, once, twice, three times. And stuff starts to freeze.

There's a cracking sound and the water round the boat turns to ice. Mitch thwacks her tail up and down, beating it away from us. 'I don't want you here,' she mutters. 'I want you over there!'

Suddenly she stops pounding the water and turns to us. 'Listen carefully. This ice is going to spread out to sea until it traps the *Alisha* – fantastic – but unfortunately it's also going to trap you two in this swan-thingy in the sea as well.'

'*What?*' I say.

'I know, not so good. The thing is, confession time, my magic is flipping awesome, but once I let it go, I can't really control it. So in a moment I'm going to swim like mad and get you as close to the *Alisha* as possible before you get stuck.'

'What happens then?' asks Win.

'I'm going to find warmer water and air, and you're going to get out and walk to the *Alisha*.'

'Will the fog last long enough to hide us from view?' I say.

'Probably,' she says, then she grins and dives below the water.

Mitch does swim like mad. Her tail cuts through the water so fast that it's a blur and her hair streams out behind her. We bash through the ice and water sprays up around us. The pedalo has become a speed boat. Mitch only slows down when the ice becomes too thick to smash through. Then she guides us down ever narrowing channels.

I'm not surprised when the swan's puffed-up chest hits a chunk of ice and we come to a juddering halt. Within seconds the water around us has frozen, locking us in place. The fibreglass body of the swan starts to make alarming cracking sounds and when I peer over the side I see Mitch waving at us from under a thick layer of ice. Her hair wraps round her webbed fingers and I see her blue lips mouth, 'That way!' as she points in the direction the boat is facing. Then, with a flick of her tail and a blown kiss – or maybe an escaped bubble of air – she's gone.

Now Win and I are alone in the middle of a frozen ocean. The silence is uncanny. Fog rolls over the side of the boat and the pedalo groans.

'Let's go and get Rose,' says Win, and together we climb on to the slippery ice and walk into the fog.

CHAPTER 49

We walk as fast as we can, our feet slipping and sliding. I keep my eyes fixed straight ahead, not daring to move my head in case we start walking in the wrong direction.

'Shame Hati smashed that compass,' says Win, followed by, 'Do you think *Mister Flambaygo* would help us here?'

I glance at my feet. Colourful fish swim beneath the ice and below them the dark sea stretches down and down. 'I think the fewer holes in the ice the better,' I say. 'And Win, we need to be quiet. We could be getting close.'

'Got it!' he says loudly.

'*Shh!*'

We're both relieved when a black shape rises out of the fog. It's a ship, and it's tilted to one side and trapped in the ice. A howl echoes from somewhere on the deck, and when we see the silhouette of a prowling wolf we know for certain that we've found the *Alisha*.

We run forward, hoods pulled low, until we're hidden

by the side of the ship. Then we work our way round the hull, looking for the rope Mitch promised would be hanging from her cabin window. This is how she climbs on board the ship and it's how I'm planning to get to Rose.

I feel like we've almost made a full circuit when we finally find the rope.

'Win, you stay here,' I say. 'I need to sneak on board. If there are two of us, it will be harder to hide.'

'But I'm a ninja. I'm super stealthy. I'm trained for *exactly* this kind of situation!'

'I know,' I whisper, wishing he would keep quiet, 'but you're my lookout. I need you down here. OK?'

Reluctantly he nods. I pause, listen for padding paws, then I start to climb. The rope is oily and wet, but it has knots tied along its length that help me pull myself up. Soon I'm approaching the window of Mitch's cabin.

I peer through the glass.

It's better than I could have imagined. Rose is lying on the leather sofa, her arms tied behind her back, and she's on her own. I thought I might find Hati inside, or that the cabin would be empty, but this is perfect!

I'm about to tap on the glass when I realise the window is slightly open, so I climb on to the windowsill, and drop into the cabin.

Rose's eyes fly open. 'Arthur?'

I put a finger to my lips, creep across the cabin, then slide the bolt on the door, locking us inside.

Rose sits up and stretches her arms out behind her. 'Quick. Untie me then we can get out of here!'

I rummage around Mitch's cabin until I find a penknife. Then I start to cut the ropes. Rose is fidgety and impatient, her eyes moving from the door to the window. 'Hurry up,' she says every few seconds.

While I cut through the thick knots I tell Rose what happened at Barracuda Bay, but she's barely listening to me. The second the rope falls to the ground she's on her feet and heading for the window. 'What are you waiting for?' she says. 'Let's go!'

I shake my head. 'Rose, we can't go.'

She looks at me like I'm mad. 'Of course we can. No one knows you're here. Win's waiting for us. We can be off this thing in seconds!'

'But when Hati realises you're gone she'll send her wolves after you. Running is pointless. It's what I was trying to tell you at The Bucket of Blood. The Dark, Candyfloss, Smokey, Bendy Joan – they all went away once we stopped being scared of them. You don't like cats, but you tickled Smokey's tummy until he walked off.'

Rose shakes her head with frustration. 'Arthur, how can I not be scared of a pack of wolves? Do you expect me to tickle their tummies?'

And that's when we hear sniffing at the door followed by a bark. Rose moves closer to the window.

'Forget about the wolves,' I say, although just the sound of the wolf's nails scratching the wood has made me flinch. Another wolf joins the first at the door and the scrabbling gets louder.

'Forget about them?' Rose stares at the door with wide eyes. 'Arthur, they can hurt me. They can bite!'

'No, you *love* wolves. It's not the wolves you're afraid of. Hati is your fear.'

Rose raises her chin and gives me a hard look. 'Scared of a girl with a stupid fur hat? I don't think so.'

'But she's not just a girl with a stupid fur hat, is she? She's a bully.' For a moment we stare at each other. Rose's mouth is clamped shut. She looks furious, but I know I can't stop now. 'Hati Skoll is a bully,' I say, 'just like Harriet Scott is a bully.'

'No!'

I put a hand on Rose's arm. '*Yes.*'

269

She shakes me off. 'Harriet Scott is my friend, Arthur, one of my best friends, or had you forgotten?'

There is a bang on the door followed by Hati shouting, '*Rose!*'

The door handle turns, but the lock holds.

'I worked it out when Hati called you Fish. Rose, Harriet Scott is mean, and she is not your friend.'

Now Hati is hammering at the door. 'Let me in, Rose! NOW!'

'The only way you are going to get rid of *her*,' I say, pointing towards the door, 'is by admitting that Harriet Scott is someone who scares you.'

Rose shakes her head. 'It's not true.'

'Harriet calls herself Hattie, doesn't she? They've practically got the same name: Hati Skoll; Hattie Scott. And remember when your amazing cakes got thrown around? That wasn't the Year Elevens, was it? I saw Hati stamping on your stuff in The Bucket of Blood, and I think that's what Harriet did to your cakes. Rose, we can stand up to her together.' But still Rose shakes her head. 'And you've got Mitch and Win too. They're your real friends.'

She does a quick laugh. 'So my real friends are a ninja wizard and a merwitch? Arthur, can't you see how pathetic that sounds?'

'It's not as pathetic as hanging out with a person like Harriet!'

Rose and I glare at each other across the cabin. Rose is barely containing her anger. Her chin is trembling and her hands are clenched. So are mine. It's like looking into a mirror. Hati hammers on the door and the wolves howl. Sometimes I feel like Rose and I are miles apart, hardly even brother and sister, let alone twins. But right now it's like we're the same person.

There is a deep long growl. It's coming from behind the door, but it fills the room. It makes the floor tremble. It rises up through my body. It makes my heart pound and sweat prickle my skin.

Rose's shoulders sag. 'Tell me how I can stand up to *that*, Arthur?'

'Don't think about how you fight off a pack of wolves,' I say, 'think about how you stand up to Hati. Don't accept the way she's treating you, Rose. Get angry. Show her you're not scared!'

Hati is hammering on the door so hard the wood around the hinges is starting to splinter. I run over and throw my weight against it.

'But I am scared,' says Rose.

'I know, and so am I, but I know you can do it.' I desperately search for the right thing to say, the one thing that will persuade her. 'Laugh, Rose, be funny. That's something you're good at.'

Rose reaches for the window. 'Let's run, Arthur, please!'

I want to climb out of the window with her and race

away across the ice, but I can't. 'I'm sorry,' I say, and I slide back the bolt.

There is this second where Rose stares at me, unable to believe what I've done; then the door bursts open, knocking me to the ground.

Hati steps over me, the wolves crowding round her, then she points at Rose. 'Get her!'

CHAPTER 50

The wolves jump forward and Rose grabs hold of the rope and hurls herself out of the window. Hati pushes the snarling wolves aside and jumps on to the window frame. Then she climbs down after Rose. The wolves fight to follow her, but the window must be too high for them to contemplate jumping. Whining with frustration, they dash past me and back on to the deck.

I run to the window. I've got to get to Rose before the wolves find a way off the boat.

I slip and slide down the rope. The fog has almost gone and I can see Rose running across the ice with Win at her side. Hati is following them, but she's not running. She strides along, hands shoved in her pockets. She knows her wolves are coming.

I jump on to the ice as the wolves rush round the side of the *Alisha*. They're barking, loving the chase. I'm about to run when I see something in the distance. Crowky is running towards us. I can't see the rest of the scarecrow army – they must have been left behind – but The Box is clutched in his hands. There are no shining letters, but I know that will change when he reaches us.

I hear a scream and turn to see the wolves closing in on Rose and Win.

'Rose, I'm coming!' I shout, as a huge grey wolf separates from the rest of the pack and leaps at her, paws outstretched. It lands on Rose's back, slamming her down on the ice. Then Rose and Win disappear in a knot of wolves.

I run forward. I can't see what's happening, but Hati is clearly enjoying herself. She's watching with a smile on her face. When I skid to a halt I see that Win is fighting like mad, but Rose is curled in a ball.

'Get up, Rose,' I shout. GET UP!' Then I wade into the mass of wolves, grabbing hold of their fur and trying to pull them off.

With one whistle from Hati, two of the wolves spin round, knock me down and pin me to the ice. I twist and turn, trying to escape, but they are so heavy I can barely move. Rose wraps herself into an even tighter ball.

A thud comes from underneath me. Mitch is smashing against the ice with her fists and tail. She looks furious, and as she pounds the ice again and again her hair tangles round her face and arms.

Hati walks over to Rose and the wolves fall back. They watch, jaws quivering, as Hati decides what to do next.

With a smash Mitch breaks through the ice. She pulls herself through the hole taking huge gasping breaths, then she spins round, using her tail to smack the wolves off me. They skitter backwards and Mitch and I lunge towards Rose.

Hati simply lifts her fingers to her lips and whistles again. This time the whole pack turns on us. I'm knocked down and it hurts. Teeth scrape my face and claws dig through my onesie into my skin, but it's worse for Mitch. The wolves bite at her tail, making her yell with pain. She reaches for one of the bottles round her neck, but it's no use. The wolves soon have her pinned down too. Now there's no one to help Rose.

I can barely breathe with the wolf pressing down on my chest, but I manage to shout, 'Rose, get angry. Show her who you are!'

Hati puts her foot on Rose's curled-up back and gives her a kick. 'Get up,' she says.

Rose stays where she is.

'Listen to me, Rose.' Mitch's voice is loud and clear. 'That girl needs to hear you roar.' The wolves pant over us and I can hear the thud of Crowky's feet as he runs towards us. 'Let her have it!'

Then Rose nods. It's a tiny movement and Hati doesn't see it.

Hati grabs Rose's hair, just like she grabs hold of the wolves' fur, and she shakes her from side to side. 'Didn't you hear me? I said, GET UP!'

'No.' Rose's voice is so quiet I wonder if I imagined hearing it.

Hati pulls Rose's face close to hers. 'What did you say?'

'I said, *no*.'

Hati sucks in her breath and I feel the wolves loosen their grip on me. 'This is your last chance!' Hati practically spits the words out, furious now. 'GET UP AND COME WITH ME!'

'No,' says Rose, wincing with pain. 'And you've got it all wrong. This is *your* last chance!'

Then I see something incredible happen to my sister's face. Her look of pain turns to one of rage. With a yell Rose grabs hold of Hati's ankle and pulls her down. Then she jumps to her feet and stands over her. 'You are mean to your wolves, you are rude, you shout, and you wear WAY TOO MANY STUPID TASSELS!'

Hati responds by wrapping her arms round Rose's legs and trying to drag her down.

'Feeling angry?' shouts Rose. 'Me too!'

And then they are tumbling round and round on the ice, arms and legs flying. The wolves lift their paws off me and Mitch. They step away from Win, who wriggles towards us. Mitch reaches for a vial, but I shake my head. 'She doesn't need magic,' I say. 'Look at her!'

Rose has grabbed hold of Hati's hands and is pinning them down. Hati shoots a desperate look at her wolves and manages a whistle. They growl, low and deep, but they don't move. Maybe Hati senses she's losing them because suddenly she stops struggling and instead she lies back on the ice and howls with rage.

Rose responds with a cry of her own. She screams in Hati's face and it gets louder and louder. The wolves start to whimper, tails between their legs, and they back away. Hati gets her hand free and sends a punch towards Rose, but Rose just wraps her hand round Hati's fist and forces it back down, all the time screaming at the top of her voice.

'Rose has totally lost it!' says Win.

Mitch grins. 'No, she hasn't. She's found it.'

And then a strange thing happens. It's not just a scream coming out of Rose's mouth, but glittering splinters of ice. This is no puff of frosty breath. It's like the dragons' fire, and it pours out of Rose faster and faster, until the two girls are half hidden in a storm of white. I look at Mitch and Win, wondering if they've done a sneaky spell, but they look as amazed as me.

'I *knew* she was a warlock,' whispers Win.

Rose falls silent and gets to her feet. Her billowing cloud of ice moves with her, twisting round her arms and legs. Then she stands over Hati, raises one fist in the air and yells, 'HEAR ME ROAR!' slamming her foot down on the ice.

There is a crack like thunder. I'm not sure if it comes from the ice or the sky, but I feel the ice shift beneath me and freezing water slops over my feet. I look around, dazzled. Crowky is still marching towards us, The Box held high, but he's unsteady on his feet. He slips and I realise that a patchwork of cracks is spreading across the ice like a spider's web.

Rose is still standing over Hati. She looks like a magician as her storm continues to twist higher and higher up her raised arm. Finally it breaks away from her fingertips and floats up into the sky where it forms a huge shifting shape above us. Flakes escape and drift down on my face.

Then, except for the groaning of the ice, everything is quiet.

Hati staggers to her feet. She finds her hat and pulls it down on her head. Then she whistles for her wolves.

One skulks over to her, Flea, but the rest run in different directions, jumping across the cracked ice, heading towards land. Hati watches them go then turns and trudges away. Without her wolves she looks like the girl that she is. Flea pads behind her, until they are just shadows. Then the sun shines a little brighter and she's gone.

The four of us flop down on the ice. We know we've only got moments until Crowky arrives, but we don't rush back to the boat or try to get away. We're too exhausted to move. For a few precious moments we rest, while up in the sky Rose's ice cloud continues to shift and swell.

'Hey,' Mitch says to Rose. 'You made an ice-storm.'

Rose looks up and laughs. 'I did, didn't I?'

Then Mitch scoops up some the ice, opens a vial and lets a few drops of golden liquid fall on to it. 'Dandelion juice,' she says as she pats it into a ball, 'infused with a dash of unicorn wee.' Then she tosses it towards Rose. It flies through the air, but just before it smacks Rose in the face it dissolves into sunshine.

Rose grins into the golden light. It's not a Harriet smile, it's a proper smile, and it's so big it makes her freckles stretch across her cheeks. Then Mitch laughs and shoots across the ice, pulling Rose into her arms.

CHAPTER 51

Rose and Mitch are so wrapped up in each other they don't notice what is happening around us.

The ice is breaking up. Maybe Mitch's ice spell has stopped working, or perhaps it was Rose's rage. Whatever the reason, the cracks are getting wider and chunks are floating away.

Crowky must be worried that he won't reach us because now he's half running, half flying towards us, leaping between ice floes. His wings stretch wide as he jumps and lands in front of us with a thud. Like us, he's exhausted. He takes great shuddering breaths, all the time clinging to The Box.

But the sight of me gives him his energy back. He's so close to getting what he wants. He puts The Box on the ice and smiles, knowing that the writing will appear at any moment. 'What's in the box, Arthur?' he says.

It's as if The Box has heard his words. Immediately the letters start to form, dazzlingly bright against the cardboard.

One look at Rose makes me realise that I actually want my name to appear. She's slumped against Mitch, too tired to move. I force myself to get to my feet and Win does the same.

I hear a crack behind me followed by Rose shouting, 'Arthur!'

The chunk of ice we're standing on has split in two. Mitch and Rose are drifting away from us. *They'll be fine*, I tell myself, *Mitch can push Rose to the ship*. But I'm not so sure about me and Win. We're stuck with Crowky and The Box, and the message is almost complete.

What's in the box? glows, and then I see a sweeping

'A' followed by an 'R'. The rest of my name appears with frightening speed. I can't stop this now. *I'm sorry, Grandad*, I think as Crowky's twig fingers pull back the lid. 'Take me to Home, Arthur,' he yells.

I grab hold of Win's arm, and he must feel my fear because he shouts, 'Leave my friend alone!'

Crowky pauses, the lid half open. 'Your *friend*? Wininja, how stupid are you? Haven't you ever wondered why your "friend" won't take you to Home? He's not your friend: you're his prisoner, and he keeps all of us trapped in Roar. But that's about to end!' And with this he throws open the lid.

There's nothing I can do. Mitch has dived into the sea, but she's not coming to help us, she's pushing Rose back towards the *Alisha*. 'Mitch!' I yell, but Rose's storm continues to swirl above us, sending down flurries of ice and a fierce wind. Mitch can't hear me. She can barely see me!

My stomach twists as I stare at the black opening of The Box. But nothing comes out. Ice falls on us, the wind howls. Still nothing comes out.

Just when I'm wondering if I'm safe, Win steps towards Crowky. Then, loudly and clearly he says, 'You're wrong. We're not trapped here. Anyone can get to Home. I've been there twice!'

Crowky stares at him, dumbstruck. '*What?*'

'Win, what are you doing?' I say, but it's like I haven't spoken.

Win keeps walking towards Crowky. 'I've crawled through the tunnel above the waterfall. I've visited Home. I've seen Arthur and Rose there, and their grandad, and I've seen loads of other things too.'

'But . . . how?' Crowky whispers.

'SHUT UP, Win.' I throw myself at him and try to wrap my hands round his mouth, but he pushes me aside with such force that I slide back across the ice.

'Getting into Home is easy,' he says, then he points at the T-shirt Crowky's wearing. 'You just need that, or anything that comes from Home. The T-shirt is a key that will take you there.'

Crowky lets go of The Box and the lid falls shut. The words fade away. My fear has come out.

Crowky stares down at Grandad's 'NO PROB-LLAMA' T-shirt. Then he starts to laugh.

'Arthur?' Win looks around in confusion, then rushes over, pulling me to my feet. 'Arthur . . . What have I done?' Our teeth are chattering and we're shivering. 'I'm sorry,' Win says again and again.

'It's too late,' I say. 'Look.'

Crowky has already left. He's abandoned The Box and us, and he's leaping back across the ice, heading for land. *No, not land,* I think, *he's heading for Home.*

CHAPTER 52

'Crowky's right,' says Win. 'I am stupid.'

'Listen to me, Win. It wasn't your fault. The Box made you say those things. My fear has always been that Crowky will get to Home. It could have been you saying that stuff, or me, or it could have been written with fireworks in the sky. As soon as The Box was opened it was going to happen.'

Win stares after Crowky. 'We need to do something, Arthur. Go after him!'

'There's nothing we can do,' I say. The ice floe we're standing on has shifted and we're drifting out to sea.

'There's something I can do,' says Win, eyes blazing. 'Magic!' And with that he wriggles out of his onesie and holds it high above his head. Now he's standing on the ice, in his pants once again. He takes out his wand.

'Win,' I say. 'What are you doing?'

'Only my new best spell ever,' he says, then he points his wand at Crowky and yells, 'BOGGLE HISS!'

There's a bang, a flash of black stars, and suddenly Win's onesie has vanished from his hand and instead he's clutching Grandad's 'NO PROB-LLAMA!' T-shirt.

Across the ice we see Crowky stop and spin round. He's wearing Win's fur onesie. He pulls it open and stares at his chest. That's when he realises the T-shirt has gone.

'The swapping hex,' I say. 'Win, you're brilliant!'

Win laughs with glee, yelling, 'Bad luck, Crowky!' Then he waves the T-shirt over his head and, still in his pants, he starts doing a triumphant dance. 'Who's stupid now? *You are* because you're wearing a too-tight furry onesie!'

It is too tight. Crowky can barely stand up in it. Clumsily, he struggles out of it.

Meanwhile Win has put on the 'NO PROB-LLAMA!' T-shirt and is moonwalking backwards across the ice. He points with both fingers at the T-shirt. 'Look what I've got!' he shouts. 'Oooooh yeeeaaaah!'

Crowky starts running back towards us. His wings burst open and he leaps from floe to floe with impossible speed. Win stops dancing. 'He can't reach us, can he?' he says.

Our chunk of ice is still floating out to sea, but Crowky is moving fast.

'I think maybe he can,' I say, just as Crowky makes the final jump. His wings flap and strain, his legs windmill through the air, then he lands in front of us with a crash.

He stays in a crouch. His head is down and his shoulders shake as he tries to get his breathing under control. Then, slowly, he looks up at us. 'This is where it ends,' he says, and he leaps forward and rips the T-shirt from Win's body.

This sends Win toppling backwards. His arms reach for me, but Crowky has already grabbed hold of my shoulder. A chill sweeps from his twig fingers and into my body, locking my limbs. All I can do is watch as Win teeters on the edge of the ice before splashing into the sea.

'Win!' I shout, but Crowky squeezes my shoulder so hard that my legs slip out from under me and I slam down on the ice. He hovers over me. 'Drain,' he hisses in my ear, 'drain . . .' Then he turns his head so he can watch Win struggling in the water.

'Help him,' I whisper, but Crowky just smiles. 'Too cold,' I add. My skin is cold. My heart is so cold that it hurts, but I'm talking about Win. His lips have gone blue and his head keeps sinking under the water. He tries to grab hold of the ice floe, but his fingers slip straight off. He tries again, and again. Then, just when I think he's going to give up, he manages to dig his fingertips in and cling on.

For a moment we stay like this, with Win dangling in the water and Crowky draining the life out of me. Our chunk of ice has caught in a current and this, combined with the wind from Rose's storm, is pushing us out to sea.

Win tries to pull himself up, but he keeps falling back. Eventually he stops trying and rests his face on the ice close to mine.

'Win . . . get out,' I whisper.

He shakes his head. Frost is dusted across his hair. It's turned his eyelashes white. 'Can't.'

I want to reach out and pull him from the water, but Crowky continues to press his twig fingers into my skin. I can barely move my head. I can barely talk. Win knows this and moves his hand along the ice until our fingers are just touching.

He's freezing in the water, but he's still trying to help me. He knows that the touch of a friend will stop Crowky from being able to stuff me. I feel a tingle in my hand, a tiny rush of warmth, but it's not enough.

Suddenly Crowky lets go of me and sits back. He's deathly white and shaking. I can't tell if he's too tired to drain me any more, or if he just wants to watch what will happen to Win. The T-shirt and The Box sit next to him. Two things he loves, but they're no use to him now he's trapped on the ice with us.

I try to look around. My one hope is that Mitch will come looking for us. But we've drifted even further than I realised. I can't see the *Alisha* or land. But I do see something so strange, that for a moment I stop feeling scared. Rose's ice cloud is still above us in the sky, but it's forming a shape. *Is it a horse?* I wonder. Then I see spikes appearing on its arched back. *No*, I think. *It's a dragon.*

Win hooks his finger around mine and when my eyes meet his, he smiles. I don't think he can hold on for much longer.

I swallow. I have to find the strength to talk. I have to say something that will stop Win from giving up. 'Win, listen.' My voice is a desperate whisper. It makes Crowky laugh, but I ignore him and carry on. 'Friends like us, we have a powerful magic. It joins us together, even when I'm in Home and you're in Roar.'

His eyes flicker. 'Does it work when I do stupid things?'

I nod. 'That's when it's stronger than ever.'

His finger tightens round mine and I feel warmth creeping into my hand and up my arm. Crowky doesn't seem to notice. He gets up and stands over us. He could easily kick Win back into the water or finish stuffing me, but instead he stares down at us. '*Magic?*' he sneers, then he bends close to Win's face and says, 'You really are stupid if you believe that!'

Doubt flies across Win's face and his other hand slips into the water. Now the only thing stopping him from falling into the sea is our linked fingers. 'Our magic is immense, Win . . . It's mind-blowing. It's . . .' I feel dizzy and so tired. I let my head fall back. Up in the sky Rose's ice dragon stretches out its wings.

'Better than Mitch's?' Win's voice pulls me back.

I smile. 'It's way better than Mitch's.'

This is too much for Crowky. 'Prove it,' he says.

'Can you reach your wand, Win?'

He shakes his head.

'It doesn't matter,' I say. 'We just need to say the magic

words.' He nods but I'm not sure if he's listening to me. His eyes are half closed. Frost seems to be sealing them shut. I say the first thing that comes into my head. 'The magic words are *Winthur Arinja*. When we say them together the magic happens.'

'What's your incredible friendship magic going to make?' sneers Crowky. 'A couple of stars? Some smoke? A big snowball?'

'No,' I say, and I realise that the heat has moved up my arm and is now spreading through my body. I turn and look him in the eye. 'It's going to make a dragon.' Then I squeeze Win's finger. 'Now, Win!'

Together we say, 'Winthur Arinja!'

Nothing happens. Crowky starts to howl with laughter. 'Where's the dragon, Arthur? Let me guess, it's invisible!'

I shake my head. 'It's right behind you.'

A roar tears through the sky and ice showers down on us. Crowky spins round, and there, plunging towards us, is our dragon.

Its pale-blue wings shine in the sun and its body glitters like polished glass. We can see all the way through its belly to the fire within. No. Not fire. It's a blizzard of frost and snow. It dives and its jaws snap open. It screams again and a jet of blue ice bursts from its mouth. Crowky leaps up in the air, trying to fly out of the way, but the dragon just twists its head and hits him with another blast. Crowky's wings are turning white, freezing. They can barely move.

He tries to force them up and down, but he crashes into the sea with a splash.

The chunk of ice tips and the T-shirt slips into the water. Somehow I cling on to Win. I wrap my fingers round his wrist and haul him up next to me. We hug each other, and even though Win is freezing I feel heat rush through me. My heart beats faster, the cold lump sitting inside me thaws.

Another cry makes us look up.

The dragon is soaring towards us again, but it's not getting ready to attack. Its legs are stretched out and its talons are open. It wants to pick us up. This is our chance to get out of here. I pull Win to his feet.

Crowky stares at us from the sea. His wings are spread out and his straw hair is standing in frozen spikes. Without thinking I reach out to him. 'Come with us,' I say, 'or you'll freeze!'

He looks away from me and starts reaching for something that's floating under the surface of the sea. It's the T-shirt.

'Leave it!' I yell. The dragon is almost on us. This is Crowky's only chance to get out of here. He ignores me and lunges for the scrap of fabric.

The ice dragon dives. His talons close around my shoulders and he plucks me and Win off the ice and up into the air. The Box! I reach out for it, but I'm too late. Win's already grabbed it and is holding it tight against his chest.

He looks from me to the dragon that's lifting us higher and higher into the sky.

'*Imaginary*,' he says.

CHAPTER 53

The ice dragon swoops over The End with me and Win dangling from its claws.

As we fly over mountains and icebergs Win wonders what else our friendship magic might make. He's still shivering, and his voice is hoarse, but at least he's talking. In fact, he can't stop. 'I've always wanted a dog. Arthur, do you reckon Winthur Arinja could magic up a dog? Not an ice one, but an ordinary one with fur, just so I don't get lonely when you're not around.'

'We could try,' I say as the dragon dives low over the sea and turns towards the *Alisha*. I'm keeping one eye on The Box. Win waves his hands around when he talks and right now his fingers must be numb. I really want to keep hold of that box now that we've finally got it back.

We race towards the *Alisha*. All the ice has melted and the ship is rolling free in the water.

'Look, Win. There they are!'

Mitch is in her hot tub and Rose is standing next to

her. The orangutans are lolloping about on the deck, free from wherever Hati trapped them. Rose and Mitch see us and start waving and calling out to us. We're flying over them and I can see the orangutans gazing up at us.

'Do you reckon they're staring because I'm in my pants?' asks Win.

'No,' I say. 'They're definitely looking at the ice dragon.'

Win glances at the talons that are gripped tightly around us. 'Arthur, how do you think we're going to get down from here?'

We don't need to worry. The dragon has a plan. It waits until it's directly over the hot tub then opens its claws. We hit the water with an almighty splash. The Box sinks under the surface then bobs up again. For a moment Mitch pretends she's mad at us, and starts yelling about boys contaminating her water, but then she throws her arms round us and pulls us into a hug. 'You crazy idiots,' she says. 'Where did that dragon come from?'

'We magicked it!' says Win. 'Arthur and Rose are actually pretty good magicians, Mitch. They're almost as powerful as us.'

'Give me that thing,' says Rose, reaching for The Box. Mitch passes it to her and then, with the help of an orangutan, Rose wraps a rope round it, tying complicated knots as she goes. The glowing letters haven't appeared on the side of it yet, which is strange, but I tell myself that when they do, it doesn't matter.

Crowky's not here. No one will open it.

'Room for one more?' asks Rose, then she jumps into the tub with us.

We hug in our wet onesies like two bedraggled polar bears. 'Thanks, Arthur,' she says, squeezing me. 'You know, for saving my life and everything.'

'I didn't save you,' I say. 'You did that by yourself.'

Then we stop hugging and try to dunk each other instead. Obviously Mitch and Win have to join in too, and it turns into a water fight that Mitch wins. Soon we're all warmed up and utterly exhausted, and we float around the hot tub while Win tells everyone what happened after we were swept out to sea.

It's fair to say he uses a lot of exaggeration. In his version of events he fell off the ice floe doing an 'epic flying tiger kick' and would have died if he didn't have fingers 'like steel'. By the time he's describing the moment we cast the winthur arinja spell even the orangutans have gathered round to listen.

'So where's Crowky now?' asks Mitch.

'We left him in the sea,' I say. 'I tried to get him to come with us, but he refused.'

We talk about what we should do, and if we should go looking for him. It's Mitch who makes the final decision. 'I'm captain of this vessel,' she says, 'and I've got to look after my crew. Look at Win. He's still blue! I need to make him a potion and get us to warmer waters. Plus, this ocean is vast. Where would we even start looking for him?'

I know she's right, but as she pulls herself out of the hot tub and disappears into her cabin I still scan the waves for any sign of Crowky. It feels wrong to leave anyone out here.

Mitch reappears with blankets and a red smoking potion for Win to drink. We heave our aching bodies out of the hot tub and start to dry off. Win ties one of the blankets round his waist like a sarong and then downs the potion in one go. 'Arthur, look at me!' Smoke is pouring from his nostrils and when he opens his mouth it rolls out over his tongue. 'I'm a dragon!'

Rose pulls her blanket tight round her shoulders and frowns. 'Arthur, what day is it?'

I do a quick calculation. I know we arrived at the Vampire on Tuesday, but after that everything went a bit hazy. Time doesn't mean much in Roar. 'Thursday?' I say.

'Then we need to go. Mum and Dad are expecting to pick us up on Sunday, and we don't know how long it's going to take us to sail back!'

'I've got this,' says Mitch and she starts bellowing instructions to her crew. She includes Win, much to his delight, telling him to go on watch in the crow's nest.

'Coming, Arthur?' he says as he starts to climb the rigging.

'In a minute,' I say. Unlike him, I've not drunk a fire potion and my legs are still wobbly.

Just then the ice dragon's shadow falls over us. Ever since it dropped Win and me in the hot tub it's been circling the boat, sending out blasts of ice.

'Look at our dragon, Arthur!' shouts Win. Then he continues climbing up to the crow's nest.

I turn to Rose. 'You won't tell him it's your dragon, will you?'

She shakes her head. 'You two deserve this one.'

I've been thinking about the ice dragon and how it formed from the ice that poured from Rose when she screamed. 'You made it back at Grandad's, didn't you?'

Rose nods. 'I think so. I found that dragon toy when you went downstairs and just for a moment I imagined it was huge and sculpted from ice . . .'

'And then when you screamed it came to life,' I say.

Rose smiles. 'Maybe at The End I have to scream for dragons instead of whistling for them.'

'Shame you didn't know you could scream for a dragon earlier,' I say. 'Like back at the Vampire when Hati climbed out of The Box.'

Rose grins. 'But then we wouldn't have had our adventure, Arthur, and I wouldn't have missed this for the world.'

Neither would I, I think as the *Alisha* swings round and begins to cut through the waves. Then, standing together, Rose and I watch the ice dragon as it loops through the sky.

CHAPTER 54

I sleep for most of the journey home. And eat. Mitch and Rose use the time to catch up, and whenever I come on deck for some fresh air I find them whispering in the hot tub as if they're plotting something. They hang out in Mitch's cabin too. Occasionally puffs of coloured smoke seep out from under the door accompanied by wild laughter.

Thanks to Mitch's M.O.O.N. magic we cross the Bottomless Ocean in record time and on Saturday, just as the sun is beginning to set, we reach land.

The Lost Girls must have seen us coming because they're waiting for us on the beach. When Mitch spots Stella she mutters, 'Urgh, Stella the mushroom thief.' Then she gasps. 'I think my memory's come back!'

We decide this is a good reason to celebrate; well, this and having found The Box and got rid of Hati and Crowky. The orangutans fetch the Lost Girls in rowing boats and then provide the music. Orangutans, we discover, are excellent fiddle players. While their wild music plays, the

Lost Girls rampage over the boat. They climb the rigging, swing in the hammocks and generally drive Mitch mad.

'Oi! The hot tub is BANNED!' she shouts on more than one occasion.

Still, even a couple of Lost Girls in the hot tub isn't enough to ruin Mitch's good mood. She's nearly home and she knows it. We decide that tonight Rose and Mitch will sleep at Mitch's hut while Win and I go back to his cave. Then we will have one whole day to explore Roar.

As the stars come out, the Lost Girls start having races to the top of the rigging and the 'grown-ups' – Win, Mitch, Stella, Rose and me – sit around the hot tub. Mitch is in it, of course.

The Box is on the deck next to us. We've been keeping it close during the journey, watching for any sign of the message, but so far we haven't seen a glimmer of magical light. It's just dull, plain cardboard.

'So what are you going to do with this thing?' asks Win, patting The Box. It's still wrapped in Rose's tangle of ropes, and Mitch added some magical super-strong seaweed. It looks like something that's been dragged up from the bottom of the ocean.

'I say we take it to Home,' says Rose.

I shake my head. 'It won't fit through the tunnel.' During the journey, I've been thinking a lot about The Box, and I think I might have come up with a solution. 'I say we try to open it.'

'*What?*' The others stare at me open-mouthed.

'Arthur, this box has given us nothing but trouble,' says Rose. 'We need to get rid of it.'

'We can't get rid of it,' I say, 'and I don't think we need to. Since we left The End, the message hasn't appeared, and something else has changed: I'm not scared of it any more.'

'Really?' says Win.

I nod because it's true. I realised it as we sailed back through the gap in the mountains. I was sitting on The Box watching Win do some kicks. The Box was uncomfortable, what with all the rope and seaweed, so I pushed them to one side, and just like that, I realised I wasn't frightened of it.

'If this trip has taught me anything,' I say, 'it's that everyone is scared of something, but when you've got friends, real friends, those fears lose their power. Rose, I think you know this too, and that's why the message hasn't appeared. It's not *The* Box any more, it's just a box.'

'Arthur's right,' says Win. 'Friends like us have a powerful magic. We can make dragons!'

'So we just . . . open it?' says Rose.

I nod. 'And we leave it open.'

She frowns. 'But what if you're wrong? What if something does come out?'

'If we've got each other, we can face anything.' I look straight at Rose as I say this. 'I want her to know that what we have in Roar, this magic, will follow us home.

'I'll always be there for you, and you'll always be there for me, right?'

The light from the stars shine on Rose. She smiles and shrugs. 'Of course. You're my brother.'

'Then let's do it,' I say.

Everyone gathers around. The orangutans stop playing their music. The Lost Girls come down from the rigging. Win helps us pull off the layers of rope and seaweed until The Box is sitting in front of us, its lid loose.

Rose puts her hands on it. No glimmering letters appear. 'It's just a box,' she says, then she pulls the lid open, and together we look inside.

Right at the bottom I see a tuft of grey fur. I take it out and let it float out of my hands. 'It's empty,' I say.

Then the Lost Girls cheer, the orangutans start playing their music again, and Win makes everyone laugh by climbing into The Box and dancing.

'This is a serious dance,' he protests. 'Stop laughing!'

CHAPTER 55

'So, mate.' Win and I are having breakfast on the rock outside his hut. 'You've got one day left in Roar. What shall we do?'

I gaze at the rivers and waterfalls and mountains that all need exploring. Then I remember that Win and I have unfinished business.

'I want to ride a unicorn,' I say.

He smiles. 'Nice . . . More toast?' I nod and he reaches into the box next to him and pulls out two jars. 'Marmite or honey?' he asks.

The Box has become Win's store box. It's full of bread and swords and comics, and his last few precious pieces of pick 'n' mix. It's already got a bit crumby and battered. I'm not sure how long it's going to last.

'A bit of both,' I say.

Once we've eaten our breakfast we spend the rest of the day looking for female unicorns, and in the end we discover two eating sunflowers in a meadow. They're bigger than male unicorns and possibly even more beautiful. One is blue with a purple mane, the other one is grey with silver spots. Their horns are the same glittery, luminous white.

This time we're not taking any chances. We sit on the floor and wait for them to come over to us. First they sniff us. Then the blue one scratches my hair with her horn and then, only after we've given them a whole sack full of apples, are we allowed to sit on their backs.

'Look at us, Arthur,' says Win as we trot towards the On-Off Waterfall. 'We're riding unicorns!'

I stroke my unicorn's sleek neck. In my head she's called Ronaldo and we're the best of friends.

Rose is impressed to see us turn up on unicorns, although she tries to hide it. 'I prefer a bit more height,' she says. She's riding Prosecco and it is true that he's slightly bigger than the unicorns. 'Cool horns though,' she's forced to admit.

Of course Mitch can't come to the waterfall to see us off so it's just Win who leads us up the rocks to the tunnel.

'Come back soon,' he says, hugging me tight, 'and bring more rocky road.'

I hug him back. 'Don't go near any icy water without me,' I say. 'And give Ronaldo some apples if you see her.' I admitted that I'd given my unicorn a name when Win told me his was called Penguin.

Win insists on sending Mister Flambaygo ahead of us into the tunnel to light our way.

Mister Flambaygo does light our way. The ball of fire is so dazzling we can barely open our eyes as we crawl towards Home. It also makes the rock red hot to touch so it's a relief when we reach the mattress and the globe fizzles out and vanishes from sight. We tumble on to the attic floor, me first, and then Rose, and for a moment we just sit there, dazed.

Grandad is on the sofa waiting for us. He's got a cup of coffee in his hand and he's wearing his slippers and his usual shorts. A newspaper is open on his lap. It's a brilliantly normal sight.

He grins. 'You cut it a bit fine. Did you have fun?'

'I think we had our best adventure ever,' I say.

He takes in our bruised and dirty faces, and our tatty clothes. Rose pokes a finger through a burn hole in her onesie.

'Excellent!' he says.

CHAPTER 56

We just have time to have a shower and to get our stories straight before Mum and Dad arrive to pick us up. This time we don't blame our cuts and bruises on a bike accident, but on an epic clear out at the allotment.

'I told them to watch out for those brambles, but there was no stopping them,' says Grandad.

Back at home Rose tells me more about Harriet. She shows me her phone and all the screen shots she's saved from Instagram and Snapchat. On one, *hattie_scottie* has posted a picture of a dead fish floating in a rock pool and written:

reminds me of *rosietrout.x.xo_x* lol

rebel1234_x you mean . . . but true!!

sophiedreamz wat if she sees it

hattie_scottie truth hurts!!! only joking tho

There are lots more like this.

A spotty dog with an ugly face with *hi Fish* written below it; a selfie Rose took of herself on the beach captioned *couldn't be happier!* which is then followed by a string of sarcastic comments from Harriet – *stunning! #instamodel* – and a picture of Rose's friends all drinking milkshakes with Harriet in the centre, with the comment *ooops forgot to invite the Fish!!!*

Nearly every one of these picture and comments starts with Harriet. No, not Harriet, Hattie. It makes me furious. I want to show Mum and Dad and our teachers. I want to join Instagram and write cruel comments below every single one of Harriet's selfies. I can't do this though. For one thing, I don't have a phone, but more importantly Rose doesn't want me to.

'So what *are* you going to do?' I ask.

'First of all, this,' she replies, and in front of my eyes she deletes all her social media accounts. She keeps the screenshots though, just in case she ever needs them.

'Is that it? What about at school on Monday?'

She smiles, and her hand goes to the small glass bottle she's been wearing round her neck ever since we got back from Roar. 'I've got it sorted, Arthur. Mitch taught me a spell and it's all I need. Oh, and you. If you don't mind me hanging out with you and Adam Zeng for a while, that would be good.'

I look at the bottle. 'Rose,' I say, 'what're you planning to do?'

'I'm going to teach Harriet a lesson.'

'What sort of lesson?'

But Rose refuses to say any more.

* * *

Walking to school on Monday feels different. For one thing, Rose hasn't got her phone in her hand. I've hardly seen it since we got back. Instead she's clutching Mitch's glass bottle.

'I really wish you'd tell me what's in there,' I say. 'If you're going to make Harriet disappear in a hurricane or get frozen into a block of ice, I'd like to know about it.'

She looks at me and smiles. 'Stop being such a funge, Arthur. It's just a bit of sea urchin ink mixed with cloudberry juice. Oh, and a dash of paprika.'

'But what does it do?'

'You'll find out in a minute.'

Rose is speaking calmly, but I know how difficult this if for her. She's been tense all morning and the only thing that seems to be helping her is the small bottle. As we approach the school gates we see Harriet in her usual spot, leaning against the fence with a group of girls.

They look up when they see us coming. Harriet smiles at one of the other girls and gives her a nudge. Suddenly it's obvious to me what she's doing; I can't believe I didn't see it before.

'Hi,' Rose says, then she walks straight past them. She's going so fast that I have to run to catch up with her. *Maybe that was it*, I think as we walk into school. Maybe all Rose had to do was stand up to Hati Skoll and then her problems with Harriet would fade away!

'Oi, Fish!' Harriet's voice rings out across the playground, loud and rude.

Rose stops walking. We turn round.

Harriet is still flanked by the girls. Some of them are staring at Rose, just like Harriet is. But not all of them. Nisha is on the edge of the group. She's fiddling with her blazer and looking at her feet. As usual all the girls have their hair in one long plait, but today Rose's hair is in a bunch. 'What's the matter with you?' says Harriet. 'Why didn't you answer any of my messages in the holidays? And what's with the hair?' She reaches forward to tug at Rose's bunch. Then she laughs.

Rose goes to step back, but then I see something flicker across her face and she stays where she is. 'I didn't answer any of your messages because I didn't want to,' she says.

Harriet's eyes narrow. '*What?*'

Rose shrugs. 'I looked through the stuff you've said about me on Instagram, and I remembered what happened with the cakes, and the way you always call me "Fish" even though you know I hate it, and I realised that you're a horrible person. Why would I want to hang out with a horrible person?'

Harriet gasps and puts her hands to her mouth. 'That's so *mean!*' she says, and her bottom lip actually wobbles. The girls who are standing closest to her put their arms round her and stare at Rose accusingly.

'No, *you* are mean,' says Rose. She's trying to keep her voice calm, but it's getting louder. She pulls out her phone. 'I've kept every single thing you ever said about me and I will show someone if I have to!'

The lip wobbling vanishes as quickly as it appeared.

Harriet steps closer. 'Do you know what, Rose? No one ever wanted to hang out with you. I had to make them.'

'Whatever,' says Rose, then she turns away from Harriet and starts to walk across the playground. Nisha, I notice, walks away too, and a couple of the other girls run after her.

I catch up with Rose.

But Harriet hasn't finished. 'Who are you going to sit with in lessons, Rose?' she shouts. 'What will you do at lunchtime, because you're not going to be with us!' Rose keeps walking. 'And you're not coming to my sleepover, or to town with us. And I'm deleting you from the WhatsApp group. NO ONE LIKES YOU, ROSE!'

This makes Rose stop in her tracks. Calmly she unscrews the bottle and shakes the pink powder into her hands. It's dotted with gold that shines in the sun. It looks like magic and it really doesn't belong in our scruffy playground. Harriet is busy tapping away on her phone and the rest of the girls, the ones who haven't left, are hovering uncertainly around her.

'Oh yes they do,' whispers Rose, and then she lifts her hand to her lips.

'Are you sure about this, Rose?' I say, wondering if I should knock the powder out of her hands. 'You're not going to hurt her, are you?' I think of the storms Mitch can conjure up, the hurricanes, the flashes of lightning that can set fire to trees.

But already Rose is blowing the powder into the air. If you didn't know it was there you wouldn't notice it.

It floats across the playground, a trail of sparkling dust that twists and turns, stopping directly over Harriet's head. It's her own little whirlwind, a pink storm waiting to break.

Then Rose whispers a word and I hold my breath.

The spell falls on Harriet. As it falls it changes. It becomes a beam of pure golden light.

Harriet lifts up her face. The other girls haven't noticed it – I don't think they even know it's there – but Harriet has. The light bathes her face and she can't help smiling. It's a big happy smile. It's not something I've ever seen Harriet do before. The light continues to fall on her, dazzling, beautiful; it's like a little piece of Roar has appeared in Home.

'Mitch gave me that powder in case I missed her,' says Rose. '*That's* what it feels like when we're together. Now Harriet knows what it's like to have a real friend.'

Then she puts the cork back in the bottle and slips it into her pocket.

'Harriet would never have done that for you,' I say.

'Exactly,' says Rose, and together we walk into school.

Rose and Arthur are back in Roar, on a voyage that
takes them further than they've ever been
before: beyond The End.

It's an amazing adventure – full of secrets, surprises
and fairies with fangs – but a mysterious storm
changes everything.

Shipwrecked on a strange island, they make a shocking
discovery . . . Could this be the end of Roar?

Don't miss the thrilling finale in the
bestselling Roar series.

The
LAND
of
ROAR
3

Coming Soon